Noon Skate

By
Carol Mackela

Noon Skate ©2017 Carol Mackela

This book is a work of fiction. Names, characters, places and incidents are products of the author's imagination or are used fictitiously.

First printing

Cover Design by Cindy Bauer
Interior Design by Cindy Bauer

ISBN-13: 978-1979177320

ISBN-10: 1979177325

Printed in the United States of America

In Memory of My Dad, a Yooper

Acknowledgments

The author would like to thank the following:

Mandy Whalen for reading the first draft and providing comments;

Valentine Wilber for editing the second draft;

Amy and Mia for dog ideas;

Ann Arbor Figure Skating Club ice dancers for hooking me on dance; and

Fred Martin, my coach, for getting me through my golds.

Chapter One – March, 2015

Monica Jones pulled her blond hair back into a ponytail and laced up her skates quickly. She was on her lunch hour from a law firm in downtown Center City, Michigan, and did not want to waste a minute of ice time. She put on her skate guards, grabbed her warmup jacket and made her way from the lobby to the rink, where several skaters were already stroking around the ice, warming up their knees by pushing with one foot and then the other.

"Hey," she said to Janet and Julian, who were skating past, hand in hand. Monica removed the skate guards from her skates, placed them near the entrance gate, and stepped onto the ice. She did a few stretches on the hockey boards encircling the rink and then began to stroke around slowly, counterclockwise, along with the other skaters. She had been skating for six years, and at age 37, her knees felt decades older, but she knew the stiffness would disappear after she had warmed up for a few minutes.

Monica had been hooked on skating since she took beginning adult skating lessons and came to enjoy the sensation of moving freely across the ice. One day after her class, she had stayed to watch an ice dance test session, where she saw skaters of all ages performing what looked like ballroom dancing on the ice – waltzes, foxtrots, tangos. Inspired, she hoped she would be able to skate that well one day, and now, here she was, working on gold level ice dances, the highest test level in the United States Figure Skating ("U.S.F.S.") ice dance hierarchy (see Appendix). She had breezed through the first two levels – preliminary and pre-bronze – in her first year of private lessons. The next year, she passed all three bronze dances and one pre-silver dance, while failing the other two pre-silvers. Though disappointed, she had reapplied herself and improved her skating, successfully testing the other two pre-silver dances in her third year of skating, and the three silver dances the following year.

With each test level, a panel of three certified judges expected to see deeper edges, more flow across the ice, and better expression of the dances. Thus, it took Monica a year and a half to pass the four pre-gold dances. She failed each of them one or two times, which was not uncommon at that level, before she was successful. She had now been working on her gold dances for six months and hoped to pass them at test sessions over the next two years, and thus, become a U.S.F.S. gold dance medalist, akin to a black belt in martial arts.

"You made it," said Brad, her friend and frequent skating partner, catching up to her on the ice. Brad Peltonen skated every day at noon, as he had for the last four years – ever since he sold his software development company and could now pick and choose the projects he wanted to work on from his home in Center City. Now 39, his passion for skating was the main focus of his life. He took Monica's hand and they stroked together around the rink, joining the other ice dancers on the public dance session. Brad, slender with light brown hair and six inches taller than Monica, matched her well on the ice. Their coach, Harvey Loomis, in his late forties, was teaching Callie, a young adult ice dancer, but he took a moment to say hello to them. He would be teaching them later in the week. Monica would be partnering Brad through his lessons and serving as his partner when he tested his pre-gold ice dances at a Center City Skating Club test session.

Monica loved the feel of gliding across the ice. By bending her knees, bringing her feet together and pushing against the ice with one foot, then transferring her weight to the other foot, she could glide half the length of the rink on her skating foot. When she reached the end, she would do crossovers or progressive running steps around the end of the rink, push onto one foot again and glide down the other side of the rink, first on one foot and then the other. She and

Brad did this exercise together and then split apart to warm up with consecutive outside, then inside edges, both forward and backward, carving half circles into the ice as they leaned into each circle and bent their knees to effectuate deeper edges.

Someone put on the music for the Fourteenstep, a pre-silver level dance that Brad and Monica had passed several years ago -- a good dance to warm up with. They started out standing side by side, did their introductory steps and Monica turned to get into dance position, similar to ballroom dancing. She would skate backwards, and Brad, forwards, for the first half of the dance. Then she would step forward, Brad would turn, and they would skate across the end pattern together before Monica would turn again and they would repeat the dance – until they got tired or someone got in their way. Skaters doing the dance being played had the right of way, but there was always someone who wasn't paying attention, so Monica and Brad had learned to watch out for each other, whichever one of them was going forward.

"Good warmup," Monica said. "Now I have to work on my golds. I have a lot to improve on." Brad nodded and skated off to work on his own dances, the pre-golds. He hoped Monica would skate a few of them with him before she went back to work.

Monica skated the Viennese Waltz, one of the four gold level dances, without the music, watching out for Harvey and his student Callie, who were skating to the music for Callie's silver level Tango. Monica loved waltzes and had a good feeling for them from her year of teaching ballroom dancing at the Williams Dance Studio in Center City before she started skating. The Viennese Waltz on the ice was fast, just as it was on the ballroom floor, and timing was critical, especially on the forward and backward progressives which Harvey had drilled her on during her last lesson. He had told her that many people fail the Viennese when they test it because of incorrect timing on the progressives. She was determined to get them right.

When she had a chance, Monica slipped a CD into the rink-side player. Harvey had prepared a CD containing the music for her four gold dances. Each dance had a prescribed number of beats per minute, and the ice dancers needed to practice to music at the correct tempo. Monica selected the music for the Viennese Waltz from the CD and hurried to take her position on the ice. She waited for the correct beat of the music to begin her introductory steps and skated two patterns of the dance – twice around the rink. She stopped to catch her breath, and then she repeated the process. Brad had been right behind her, skating the man's steps about two measures back, to give her some space.

Janet and Julian had also joined in, skating the Viennese Waltz together as a couple. They had tested and passed all twenty-three dances in the U.S.F.S. Rulebook, from preliminary level through gold, and loved to do them together, as they had for thirty years. A married couple, retired from their teaching positions at Mid-Michigan University, they enjoyed coming out to noon skate two or three days a week and doing the dances for fun and exercise.

They were always willing to help out any new skaters who were trying to learn the dance patterns. In addition, they were certified silver level ice dance judges working on their gold dance judging appointments.

Monica finished her solo Viennese Waltz and skated to the end of the rink to work on a few steps that she felt she had done poorly. Then she went on to another gold dance, the Argentine Tango. She had taught American style tango to her ballroom students and loved every style of tango -- on the floor and on the ice. The most difficult step for her was the twizzle, a 360-degree turn on one foot, done alongside the man. She worked for several minutes on twizzles at the end of the rink, out of the way of other skaters. Then someone put on the music for the Argentine, and several skaters lined up.

Couples were allowed to go first, but Brad knew not to ask Monica for the Argentine because she was working on her solo, which she would need to perform when she tested the dance, after doing it with Harvey. Monica waited her turn, listened for the correct beat, and off she went. She completed two patterns in time to the music but knew that some steps were sloppy, especially the twizzle. She looked forward to her next lesson with Harvey, hoping that he could help her clean it up.

Glancing at the clock, Monica realized it was time to go back to work and got off the ice. She took off her skates, dried the blades thoroughly with an old towel and placed the skates in her skate bag. Brad had just gotten off the ice and was unlacing his skates. "Sorry I didn't have time for pre-golds," Monica apologized. "Let's work on them tomorrow."

"No problem, see you tomorrow," he said, as Monica grabbed a sandwich that she had packed in her bag and took a bite.

She waved goodbye and headed out to her car, a small green Chevy Cruze. Her office at the Carter Day law firm was only a mile away in downtown Center City, and she arrived just as Marcia Day, one of the partners, was leaving for lunch. Monica hoped she had not stayed out too long. Marcia, a runner, understood that her employees would be more productive if they engaged in any type of exercise, and thus, she encouraged them to run, skate, walk, swim or do whatever they needed to do, as long as they got their work done.

Monica enjoyed her job as a paralegal at Carter Day, one of the biggest law firms in Center City. She had started there eleven years ago as an administrative assistant, helping out with typing and filing documents. Marcia Day and Ray Carter had realized her potential and offered her a scholarship to attend Center City Community College and then, Mid-Michigan University, to complete her Bachelor's degree in paralegal studies. With a young daughter at home, Monica could not attend classes full time, so it took her six years to complete her course work, but she finished it, and was very proud of herself for sticking with it and getting the grades necessary to keep her scholarship and earn her degree. Ray and Marcia knew their investment in Monica would pay off. She was a hard worker and a quick study, just as she had been in her ballroom teaching.

Monica parked in the lot behind the firm, which occupied the top three floors of a five-story office building. She left her skates in the car as she usually did, because she would need them again for the next day's noon skate. She took the elevator up to her office on the top floor, where she had a nice view from her large window of downtown Center City to the north, and the Center County Courthouse just a block away. Her office was small but private, and she could get a lot of work done there – far more than in the cubicle she had for the first six years. She opened a file on her desk, reviewed the legal research she was doing for Marcia on a contract dispute case, sat down at her computer and went to work. Marcia wanted the most recent and relevant cases that the Michigan courts had decided in cases similar to theirs. Monica was a skillful legal researcher, and the attorneys at Carter Day knew that they could always count on her to find relevant cases, or cases "on point," quickly.

Monica's research on a legal database was interrupted when Audra Lahti, one of the associate attorneys who specialized in civil litigation, poked her head in the door, which Monica had left cracked open. "Do you have a moment?" Audra asked.

"Sure," Monica said. She pointed to the plain, straight-backed chair next to her desk, and Audra sat down.

"I got a call from Bob Ritter, one of our clients, this morning," Audra began. "He was very upset about some kind of letter he received from the government. I think one of his employees is accusing him of discrimination. I told him to come in and bring the letter. Are you available to sit in? I know it's short notice, but he mentioned some kind of deadline in the letter. We need to know what this is all about, sooner rather than later."

"Sure, I can help," Monica said. "I'm just finishing up something for Marcia. What time is Mr. Ritter coming in?"

"Four o'clock, my office. See you then, and thanks!" Audra left and Monica went back to work.

At 3:50, Monica printed out the cases she had found for Marcia, highlighted the pertinent sections and wrote a few notes of her own in the margins. She put the cases in a file folder and left them on Marcia's desk. Then she grabbed a yellow legal pad and a pen and headed for Audra's office just down the hall.

Ritter had just arrived and was seated in the lobby. The receptionist, Anna, provided him with a cup of coffee. A few minutes later, Audra appeared and escorted her client back to her office. Ritter, the owner of a large retail furniture store, had been a client of Carter Day for years. The firm had handled tax issues, contract disputes and labor issues for him. Ritter took a seat across from Audra, and she introduced him to Monica.

"What can we do for you, Mr. Ritter?" Audra asked. "Did you bring the letter you told me about this morning?"

Ritter handed Audra the letter, and gave a copy to Monica. "It came by certified mail and I didn't get it until about two weeks after it was sent. They say I need to give them a response by next week but I don't see why I need to do anything. I haven't done anything wrong. Am I being sued, or what?"

Audra and Monica took a few minutes to read over the two-page letter, on letterhead stationery from the United States Department of Justice ("DOJ"), Civil Rights Division, Office of Special Counsel for Immigration Related Unfair Employment Practices ("Office of Special Counsel") in Washington, D.C. The letter informed Mr. Ritter that Sarah Ahmed, a lawful permanent resident alien, alleged that she had been denied a job as a salesperson because she was not an American citizen, in violation of the Immigration and Nationality Act, which prohibits discrimination on the basis of citizenship status. The letter requested that Ritter provide the Office of Special Counsel with a response to the allegations and copies of pertinent documents, such as the ones Ms. Ahmed had submitted to his company during the hiring process. At this point, his cooperation was voluntary, but the letter stated that a subpoena could be obtained. The letter was signed by Frances Warren, an attorney in the Office of Special Counsel.

"This is a notice letter, Bob," Audra said slowly, still scanning the contents of the document. "No one is suing you - yet. Ms. Ahmed has filed a charge of discrimination and DOJ is required to investigate it. I know there are two sides of every story, and so does DOJ. You want them to hear your side of it, I'm sure. Do you want us to prepare a response?"

"Can you do it by the deadline?" he asked. "What will happen if I don't do anything? I still think this is ridiculous. I have never even met this Ms. Ahmed."

Monica spoke up, directing Audra's attention to the deadline which was coming up in three days. "Maybe we could ask for an extension. I could call Ms. Warren and see what she says, at least."

"We'll take care of this, Bob," Audra assured her client. "Monica will ask for a reasonable extension and we will let you know what it is. Then we will need to talk to your employees who were involved in the decision not to hire Ms. Ahmed and find out what happened, so we can advise you on how to proceed. Is that okay with you?"

Ritter nodded his approval and Monica walked him out to the elevator. "I'll be in touch with you," she said.

Monica and Audra talked for a few minutes, and Monica went back to her office to gather her thoughts before dialing the direct line for Frances Warren in Washington. She got a recording and left a message, stating who she was and what she wanted – a three-week extension, because they had only received the letter today from their client. She hoped Ms. Warren would get back to her soon. By this time, it was 5:30, and Monica decided it was time for her to go home. She always tried to be there within a reasonable hour to spend some time with her daughter, Suzanne, now a senior at Center City High School.

As she drove to her apartment building on the south side of town, Monica wondered if Suzi had made her decision about where she would go to college in the fall. This was March, and Suzi had been accepted at the University of Michigan in Ann Arbor, Michigan State University in East Lansing, Mid-Michigan University in Center City, and

Winter College, a small private liberal arts college in Winter Grove, about 90 minutes north of Center City. Suzi was excited about going away to college – she was ready to leave home and spread her wings, and Monica would support her decision, though she knew she would miss her daughter. All of the colleges had offered scholarships that would cover books and tuition, but Winter College was the only one that offered to cover room and board, the biggest expense. Monica hoped that Suzi would choose to go there so as not to be saddled with thousands of dollars in student loan debt. Suzi had no idea what she wanted to study, so Winter College would give her a broad education that she could hopefully apply to many careers.

Monica pulled into the parking lot at Southside Apartments, a large apartment building with three floors and a large grassy area next door with playground equipment and picnic tables. She and Suzi had moved to Southside three years ago when their basement apartment on the east side of Center City was flooded. The landlord offered to let the tenants in the flooded apartments out of their leases, and Monica was fortunate to find a vacant second floor apartment at Southside. She had lost a lot of important papers and personal items and did not want to go through another flood. Now she and Suzi were high and dry in a building with a diverse group of friendly tenants, though she did not know all of the residents who occupied the 120 apartments.

The parking spaces near her end of the building were filled, so Monica parked near the main entrance, where she could run in and check her mailbox. As she was pulling out the usual handful of junk mail, she noticed one of her neighbors, Horace Raines, on his way out. Horace, a tall black man with graying hair, lived on the third floor at the other end of the building. He always had a friendly smile and today was no different. "Have a good evening, Monica," he said, and she wished him the same.

Monica took the steps up to the second floor and made her way down the long hallway, divided by several sets of fire doors which were usually propped open during the day but closed by the management at night. The building was an older one, with no sprinkler system, but tenants were urged to make sure they had working smoke detectors in their apartments, and Monica had just changed the battery in hers.

As she neared her apartment, her neighbor from across the hall, Rose Hernandez, was headed for the laundry room with a basket piled high. Rose, a nurse at Central Hospital, had two young boys, eight and ten, who often got their clothes dirty from playing outdoors every night until dark. She often complained to Monica that she could not keep up with all the laundry – there was just no end to it.

Suzi had dinner on the table – the smell of spaghetti sauce wafted through the air as Monica opened her door and stepped inside the apartment. "What a nice surprise!" she said, glad she had not stayed at work any longer. Suzi had done a great job, and they sat down to enjoy the meal.

"Guess what, Mom! I might have a job lined up for summer already," Suzi said. "At the 50-meter pool in Center City Park -- I have to go to a meeting and lifeguard training next week, and they will let us know after that."

"Wonderful," Monica said. "You can use the money for your college expenses." She didn't press Suzi on her college decision, but she would have to make up her mind soon. She thought it was wonderful – and a bit ironic – that Suzi, who had almost drowned as a small child when she fell off a dock at a lake, had grown to love swimming and was now earning money working as a lifeguard. After the episode at the lake, Monica had signed Suzi up for swimming lessons, which she had detested at first, but as she learned more and became a stronger swimmer, it was hard to keep her away from the water. Monica put her on an age group swim team and went to every one of Suzi's meets, where she excelled at the backstroke but wasn't bad at freestyle either. Suzi swam on her high school team, earning many team points and having a great time with the other girls. When she was old enough, Suzi took Senior Lifesaving and got a job at her high school pool. Earlier this year, she earned her Water Safety Instructor certification and taught swimming every Saturday morning at the same pool. The outdoor 50-meter pool would pay a bit more, however, and Suzi would enjoy being outside.

Then again, maybe all of this was not surprising considering that Suzi's father had been a champion high school diver. Maybe aquatic sports were in her blood. Monica had dated her high school crush, Randy Noonan, for a few months their senior year and Monica found out she was pregnant just before graduation. Suzi was born in February of the following year. Randy had chosen not to be part of their lives. Monica often thought that was his loss, but she went on with her life and did not hold it against him. Any time Suzi had questions about him, Monica answered as best she could, but the subject did not come up often.

Suzi went to her room to study, while Monica cleaned up the dinner dishes and relaxed with a book for a few hours. She watched the ten o'clock news and then went to bed.

Monica drove Suzi to school in the morning, as she often did, because Center City High School was a thirty-minute walk from their apartment. When Monica got to the office, she was relieved to find a message from Frances Warren, the government attorney. Ms. Warren granted the three-week extension. Monica called Bob Ritter and told him the news. "Would it be OK if I stopped by on Thursday and speak to your employees who dealt with Ms. Ahmed?" she asked. "And I'll need to see all of the documents that relate to her."

Ritter said he would set her up in a conference room and have his office manager available, along with any documents.

Monica turned to another assignment she had received from Wes Pauley, a first-year associate attorney, who wanted Monica to research something called "diminished value" in a case that he was preparing for trial. His assignment memo said that his client, Linda Baird, had been in a car accident with her brand-new Chevy Malibu. The other driver had been at fault. Linda wanted the difference between the value of the new car and its value after it was rebuilt, which was about half of what she had paid for her new car. The other driver's insurance company had refused to pay a single dime for diminished value, despite Wes' efforts to settle the case based on a written opinion from an expert on diminished value car cases.

Wes wanted to make sure he was on solid legal ground with Linda's case. He directed Monica to look for cases in Michigan, if there were any, to find out what the courts decided in other diminished value car cases. Monica felt sorry for Linda, who was struggling to make her car payments and was now driving a car worth about half what she had paid. "Could have been me," she thought, remembering when she had bought the Cruze, her first brand new car, and narrowly escaped an accident on her way home from the dealership last year. She started her search on Westlaw, one of the online legal databases.

At noon, Monica headed for Center City Ice Arena, looking forward to her usual skating break. She had dressed in one of her pantsuits that she wore on skating days, so all she had to do was discard the jacket and don her skating warmup jacket which was easy to move in and just the right weight for the indoor ice rink in March.

Callie Donaldson, Harvey's silver level ice dance student, was sitting on a bench, just staring at her skates on the floor by her feet, as if she couldn't bear to put them on.

"Are you OK, Callie?' Monica asked, wondering if Callie had blisters from her new skates.

"Oh, I guess," Callie said, "But I just can't get the mohawk and inside three-turn in the Tango. I was hoping to test it next month but Harvey told me it would have to wait.

NOON SKATE

How did you ever learn it?"

"Lots of practice," Monica told her. "I had trouble with that part, too, especially on the solo. Keep at it – you will get it. I'm having my own problems with the darn twizzle in the Argentine. There's always one step in every dance that is especially challenging."

With her skates on, Monica made her way quickly to the rink side, stepped on the ice and pushed with one foot, expecting to glide away, but instead, she found herself sitting on the ice. "Skate guards!" Harvey said, as he skated by with Kristy Parker, one of his bronze level students.

Monica had been distracted and had forgotten to remove her skate guards before she stepped onto the ice. When she tried to push against the ice with what she thought was her blade, she just went down – hard. "That looked painful," Brad said as he skated over to help her up. Monica was fine, though her left butt might be sore for a few days. Mostly, she was embarrassed at what was an avoidable fall, but one that every skater made once in a while.

Monica tried to extend her left leg as she warmed up, but her left buttock was starting to swell. She skated for an hour anyway, working on the Viennese Waltz and Argentine Tango, to prepare for her lesson on Thursday, and then worked on two of the pre-gold dances – the Kilian and the Blues – with Brad. They finished up with a few dances just for fun. Brad was fun to skate with and just the right size so she could get into dance positions easily with him. They did the European Waltz, a pre-silver dance that Monica thought she would never pass but had finally done so. She had partnered Brad through his European Waltz and he had passed with extra points from all three judges, so she always enjoyed doing this dance with him.

Callie put on the music for the silver Tango, and Brad and Monica skated this dance together, giving Callie plenty of room ahead of them. Brad made the mohawk and inside three-turn easy for Monica, and she suggested that he try it with Callie, to help her out. She noticed that Callie had no problem with these steps when she was with Brad, the most advanced male ice dancer who skated at noon skate. The women were used to sharing the men during noon skate and most other ice dance sessions, because women outnumbered them three to one and that was the only way the women would all get some partnering experience. Monica was fond of Brad and pleased that he shared his partnering ability with others. She tried to do the same with the men, if there were any on the ice who were looking for a partner.

Monica headed back to the office, ready to go back to work on the diminished value case. She also wanted to read up on the discrimination law that their client Bob Ritter was accused of violating. But first, she found a plastic bag, went to the fifth-floor kitchen, filled it with ice, and returned to her office. She closed the door tightly and stuffed the bag of ice in her pants, hoping it would stop the swelling in her butt. She would have to work standing up for a while.

That evening at dinner, Suzi surprised Monica by announcing her college decision. "Winter College," she said. "I liked the campus and the classes I sat in on when we visited last year. They even have a swim team, which I would have a chance to do well on. I wouldn't be competitive in the Big Ten, and Mid-Michigan doesn't have a swim team. I can always transfer if I hate Winter College, right?"

"Of course," Monica assured her. "Let's send in your acceptance and see what happens next." She was relieved that this decision had been made and they could start to plan for the fall. Finances would not be as big a concern with Winter College, but Suzi would need the money she earned in her summer job to cover her clothing, transportation and other personal expenses.

Monica iced her butt again before going to bed and slept on her side all night. Her derriere was feeling better on Wednesday. When she got to the office that morning, she called Bob Ritter to remind him that she would be at his company at 9:00 a.m. Thursday. Then she read everything she could find on the website of the Office of Special Counsel.

Monica learned that this Office had been in existence since 1987. Press releases about its most recent cases and settlements were posted, giving her an idea of what to expect. There were also several tips for employers about how to avoid discriminating on the basis of national origin and/or citizenship status, which she thought might be helpful. She had no idea what Ritter's personnel would tell her, but she hoped they were not prone to the anti-immigrant sentiment that had affected some Americans, including politicians, for the past several months.

Just then, there was a knock on the door. Audra was

stopping by to make sure Monica was prepared for Ritter. "Remember to tell them that they need to tell you the truth. Remind them that you are an extension of me, so the attorney-client privilege applies to any conversations you have with the company's decision makers."

Monica knew that – she had done similar interviews in a couple of other employment discrimination cases – one based on gender and one based on race – that were filed with the Michigan Department of Civil Rights. Both of these cases had been settled. She told Audra not to worry. She would find out what had happened, prepare a memo for Audra and draft a response to the letter from the Office of Special Counsel.

Later on, at noon skate, Brad and Monica worked on their dances, and their coach, Harvey, said he looked forward to their back-to-back lessons on Thursday. Monica would be coming from Mr. Ritter's company and would let her office know that she would be in after lunch. She went back to the office, continued her other assignments and wrote out a list of possible questions to ask on Thursday. Then she put everything about the case into an accordion file and went home.

Thursday morning, Monica dropped Suzi at school and proceeded to Ritter's furniture company, Ritter House, on Main Street. Sally, the receptionist, showed her to a conference room and handed her a folder containing the documents she had requested. "Our office manager, Janelle Walker, will be here in about fifteen minutes. Can I get you a cup of coffee?"

"Sure. Thanks." Monica sat down on one of the chairs placed around a small conference table and opened the folder. She found Sarah Ahmed's resume and employment application, detailing her ten years of experience at a furniture company in Grand Rapids where she claimed to have exceeded all of her sales goals. She listed three references, all in Grand Rapids, on the other side of the state, with their telephone numbers and addresses. Ms. Ahmed had completed other forms in the hiring process, including an Employment Verification Form I-9, on which she had indicated under penalty of perjury that she was a permanent resident alien. She provided a Michigan driver's license and an unrestricted Social Security Card to establish her identity and authorization to work in the United States. Copies of the driver's license and Social Security Card were attached to the I-9 form. The driver's license pictured Ms. Ahmed in a hijab, or headscarf, often worn by Muslim women. The employer's portion of the form was signed by Janelle Walker, indicating she had seen the original documents that Ms. Ahmed presented and the documents appeared genuine and related to Ms. Ahmed. Monica wondered why the hiring process had been aborted.

"Hi, I'm Janelle Walker," announced a short, middle-aged woman with brownish blond hair. "Mr. Ritter said you needed to talk to me."

"Yes, thank you. I'm Monica Jones, a paralegal at Carter Day downtown, and we have been asked to prepare a response to the letter Mr. Ritter received from the Department of Justice about Ms. Ahmed's claim of

21

discrimination. Did you meet her?"

"I did," Ms. Walker said.

Monica could see that Ms. Walker was nervous and tried to put her at ease. "I am not here to get you in trouble, Ms. Walker," she said. "But I need to know what happened so I can help figure out what to do from here on. Talking to me is like talking to the attorneys I work for – everything is confidential, so please do not hesitate to tell me everything that happened. Let's start at the beginning. When did you first hear from Sarah Ahmed?"

"Sarah responded to our ad in the Center City Chronicle for experienced sales people. She called and told me she had ten years' experience at a store in Grand Rapids, which I thought was great, and I invited her in for an interview. She filled out an application and told me all about the store where she worked in Grand Rapids. She also explained that her husband had been transferred to Center City, so that is why she was looking for a job here. I told her she was hired contingent on her references checking out and on Mr. Ritter's approval, and I asked her to fill out an I-9 form. She showed me her documents and I made copies to attach to the I-9 form. After she left, I looked more closely at the I-9 form and saw that she was not a U.S. citizen. I asked Mr. Ritter if that was any problem, and he said he did not want to hire anyone from another country. His nephew was injured by a roadside bomb in Afghanistan and he said he especially did not want to hire anyone who looked like a terrorist because that would hurt his business. I wanted to keep my job, so I called Ms. Ahmed and told her we could not hire her. I'm so sorry."

Monica was speechless. She couldn't believe Ritter had professed such ignorance, assuming Ms. Walker was telling the truth. Monica thanked Ms. Walker for her time and asked her to tell Mr. Ritter to come in.

Ritter sat down and folded his arms over his chest. "I will tell you again," he said defiantly. "I did nothing wrong. I never met Ms. Ahmed and even if I did, it should be up to me who I want to hire. Can you make this go away?"

"I will talk to Audra and get back to you," Monica said, not smiling, and very disappointed with this client. She did not want a confrontation and knew that her job was to find out what happened, which she had. She gathered her things and the documents Ms. Walker had provided, and left for the rink. She couldn't wait to get on the ice and get her mind off this case, which was going to be more difficult than she thought. Ritter did not seem inclined to admit any wrongdoing, but Monica was sure he had violated the law.

Soon, Monica was on the ice warming up with Brad, and Harvey joined them for Brad's half hour lesson. "Let's see the Blues first," Harvey said, and went to put on the music.

Monica and Brad took their starting positions in the middle of the rink, waited for the music, and started together and on time. They were skating well until they came to the choctaw, the most difficult turn for most skaters in this dance. They pulled apart and Harvey yelled at them to stop. He did the choctaw with Monica to show Brad how deeply he wanted him to take the forward edge going into the turn. Brad looked at him doubtfully.

"Let's try it," Monica said, and they got back into side-by-side position to skate the end pattern and then get into the choctaw. Brad took a deeper edge but then had trouble managing the choctaw.

"I'll work on it," Brad said. "That has always been the hardest part for me."

They went on to the Kilian, a fast dance that Monica and Brad had been doing together for some time. Harvey wanted to see deeper forward outside edges at the beginning of the dance. After the outside edges came some progressive steps and another choctaw, a bit different from the one in the Blues, but still a choctaw -- from a forward inside edge on one foot to a back outside edge on the other foot. Monica had to follow whatever kind of edge Brad took into the choctaw and then try to stay with him on the backward steps until they stepped forward and repeated the dance. She did stay with him but Harvey could tell it was not easy.

"This dance needs a lot of work," Harvey said. "Monica, go ahead and skate while I work with Brad on the Kilian."

Monica skated off to work on the Viennese and Argentine. Ten minutes later, Harvey skated over and took her hand. "Viennese," he said, and they skated through it without the music.

Harvey was a strong skater and Center City was very lucky to have him teaching there. He and his partner, Alice, had been national silver medalists in ice dance and members of the team representing the United States at the world championships and other international competitions. Alice taught in the Detroit area, where they had trained, and

NOON SKATE

Harvey had learned that Center City was completely without a high-level male ice dance coach. The Center City Skating Club had convinced him to teach on their morning and evening sessions and on Sunday adult night, which was primarily an ice dance session. He could also teach on the noon public dance session and the public general session that followed it, where there was usually plenty of room to teach his dance students. Within a month of when he started six years ago, Harvey was booked solid.

Harvey put on the music for the Viennese and skated the dance with Monica, who did her best to keep up with him. "I think you need to be stroking this dance out more," Harvey said. "Let me see the solo." He put on the music again and watched Monica do the dance by herself. Her pattern was not nearly as big as when she did it with Harvey.

"I know you have not been working on this dance for long," Harvey said gently, "but you need to work on stroking, aiming for more power, and then apply it to this dance."

Monica agreed to stroke as hard as she could for five minutes without stopping every day, and to try to push harder on all of her Viennese steps. Then they turned to the Argentine. Harvey gave her some useful tips for improving her twizzle, and she practiced for a few minutes before getting off the ice.

"Thanks for skating with me," Brad said. "I'm going to stay for the next session. See you Sunday night?"

Monica nodded and waved good-bye as she took a bite of her sandwich. She remembered that Brad was going to be out of town until Sunday, so she would not see him on Friday.

Back at the office, she found Audra and filled her in on the meeting with Bob Ritter's office manager.

"Go ahead and write it all up," Audra said. "I will do some research and try to figure out how to talk some sense into Bob."

Monica wrote a three-page memo detailing everything she had learned at Ritter House and took a stab at drafting the response to DOJ, which would have to be approved by Mr. Ritter and could not include privileged communications. She stated correctly that he denied the allegations of discrimination but was providing the requested documents in the spirit of cooperation. She left the file on Audra's desk and left for the day.

On Friday morning, Monica worked on the diminished value case in the morning and found that Michigan case law supported their client's position, that she was indeed entitled to the difference between what she had just paid for her new car and its value after it had been repaired. The court relied heavily on expert witness testimony as to how much in diminished value would be awarded. She wrote a short memo for Wes and put it in a folder along with his assignment memo and copies of the cases she had found. She put the folder on his desk and took off for the rink.

The first thing Monica did after she stepped onto the ice was to stroke, first gently to warm up, then all out for five solid minutes. Her quadriceps burned from the effort, so she did some stretches at the boards to try to loosen them up.

NOON SKATE

She noticed that her ankles were throbbing and had an idea why -- maybe it was time for new skates that would give her more support. Her current pair of Riedells was three years old and had seen quite a lot of use – skating every day at noon and for another two hours on Sunday nights for most of the last three years. Good ankle support was required for executing deep edges and getting power from her stroking. She had been pushing her current pair of skates to the limit because new ones were so expensive, but she knew her ankles would not be able to take the extra effort Harvey was asking of her unless she had proper equipment. When she got off the ice, she stopped by the skate shop in the Center City Ice Arena, where she had purchased the current pair of skates.

"How much would new boots cost me?" she asked Barry, who ran the shop. Monica almost fainted when he told her. And then there would be the cost of new blades, because her current ones were sharpened almost down to the soft metal, which would not hold a sharpening job for very long. Monica had dance blades which many of the ice dancers loved because they were shorter and thinner and had smaller toe picks than blades used by freestyle skaters. The shorter blades were better for the intricate footwork in the dances – they made stepping on one's own blade and falling less likely, and the thinner blade allowed for more flow on the ice. And, dancers had no need for toe picks – they could only get in the way.

Barry had a pair of Riedell Gold Star boots in Monica's size in stock, so she sat down and tried them on. Something was not right. These boots felt totally different from her old boots, and not because they were new. Barry thought that this year's design was different and produced another pair of boots made by a different company. These were even worse.

"What am I going to do?" Monica moaned.

"I can measure you for custom made boots," Barry offered. "They cost more but they will fit your feet perfectly."

"How much more?" Monica asked, wondering how she would manage the difference. When Barry told her, she gulped but told him to proceed, even though the new skates and blades would cost her more than a week's salary. She would just have to do without something else. There was no other way. "Go ahead," she told him, and he started to trace her feet on a piece of paper along with taking other measurements.

"I'll order them today," he said. "It usually takes about a month."

Monica hoped she would have the new skates in time to break them in before summer, when she hoped to be ready to test her first two gold dances. The break-in period would be at least a couple of weeks. She told Barry to also order a new pair of dance blades, and she gave him her credit card for a down payment on the new boots and blades. The balance would be due after she tried on the boots to make sure they fit. Barry would then have to waterproof the soles of the boots and mount the blades on them. Monica was thankful that she had a full-time job that would cover her skating expenses – her one extravagance, but one that she knew she could not live without.

When Monica got back to the office, Wes was coming down the hall. "Thanks so much for your help on Linda's case," he said. "There is one more thing you can do."

"Sure," Monica said. "What is it?"

"Well," Wes said, "I'm wondering if it is worth it for Linda to pursue this case. Even if she recovers the entire amount of diminished value, she would still need to pay attorneys' fees and the expert witness fees for her testimony. She would end up in the hole unless we can recover attorneys' fees from the other side. Would you research in what instances the courts have awarded them?"

Monica said yes and jotted down a few notes on the assignment. She noticed that the Ritter file was back on her desk, with a few notes and questions from Audra. She would be busy this afternoon and looked forward to Saturday when she would have some time to herself.

*****

"Do you need the car today?" Suzi asked on Saturday morning. "I have to work at the pool all day."

Monica did need the car for errands and grocery shopping, so she dropped Suzi off at the high school pool and headed for Meijer's Thrifty Acres, where she could buy gas, food and everything else she needed all in one place. She didn't know what she would do without Meijer's. When she returned home from shopping, the parking spaces at her end of the building were filled up again, mostly by a moving van that was being unloaded, so Monica parked near the main entrance and started to carry her groceries up the stairs and down the long hall to her apartment. It was still so early that the manager had not propped open the fire doors, so Monica had to open each set of them with her hands full of grocery bags. Rose's two boys were on their way out to play and offered to help hold the doors, which she thought was very nice of them. Rose would be proud.

As Monica was making her last trip in with food, she met the new family – Dr. and Mrs. Singh and their two young daughters, who would be living on the third floor. The Singhs said they were both teachers at Center City Community College. Monica looked forward to getting to know them.

Monica picked up Suzi that night when she was done working at the pool. They stopped for burgers on their way home, even though Monica had just stocked the refrigerator at home. Suzi said she was so hungry, she simply could not hold out until she got home.

Sunday night Monica went to the Center City Skating Club adult ice dance session at the Center City Ice Arena. The club session was much more expensive than public skating, but it was the only time she would see many of the ice dancers. Some of them could not get away to skate at noon and just skated on Sundays and on weeknights, during other expensive club sessions. Monica looked forward to seeing everyone and wondered how Brad was doing. He had only been gone for a day of skating but she had missed him, and not just the skating part. She had always enjoyed skating and talking to Brad, but they had never been involved off the ice – one or the other of them had always been in a relationship and unavailable, or too busy for anything except work and skating.

The Sunday session started with thirty-minute group lessons taught at three levels: beginning (preliminary and pre-bronze dances), intermediate (bronze and pre-silver dances), and advanced (silver, pre-gold and gold dances). Even though she had passed all but the gold dances, Monica still learned from the group lessons and tried to absorb any new information that was offered, such as on the man's steps and on partnering. Harvey taught the advanced group and two other coaches, Cathy and Lynn, taught the others.

After the lesson, there would be 45 minutes of programmed dances, where the order of dances could not be interrupted by the coaches or anyone else, and everyone had to do the dance being played or get out of the way. A small area in one end of the rink was marked off by small red cones to indicate it was reserved for beginners to practice on, if they did not know the dance being played. Monica had taken advantage of this practice area the first year she skated, and it was a good vantage point for watching the dancers fly past on the dances she did not yet know. By the second year she had learned the steps to all the dances in the Rulebook and could at least slop through them and get her money's worth on the Sunday session. Now after six years of lessons she was doing all the dances well and trying to help others who were learning them.

After the 45 minutes of programmed dances, there would be a resurface, or "Zamboni solo," as the skaters called it, to prepare a clean sheet of ice. The last hour would be mostly the higher dances from silver through gold. Skaters could subscribe to the first half of the session, the last half or both. Monica skated both sessions. This was the best workout she would have all week, knowing that she could do all of the dances, stopping only when the music changed and the skaters lined up for the next dance. She had fun and got almost two solid hours of exercise.

This Sunday, Harvey was teaching the advanced group the Westminster Waltz, one of the four gold dances. Monica was wondering what had happened to Brad, but he showed up, skated over to her side and listened to Harvey's comments. Brad took Monica's hand and said, "Here I am. Traffic from up north was terrible for the last three hours but I made it."

Monica would have to ask him about this during the break. Right now, Harvey was teaching the man's steps and pattern for the "West," and Brad followed Harvey and the other men in the group. Monica already knew her part, so she followed the men to see what they had to do. They had to negotiate a difficult turn called a counter, while the women performed a corresponding rocker turn. Harvey gave the group pointers on how to do the turns individually and then as a couple. He told them to practice while he went around and assisted each person or couple. Since there were more women, he asked the men if they would try that section of the dance with one of the women who had not tried it yet with a partner. No one fell, and everyone seemed to be learning.

The 45-minute programmed dance session started with

the Dutch Waltz, one of the preliminary level dances. Monica and Brad looked for beginners they could help and lined up at the end of the rink with two such skaters in tow. Monica was with Sean, a college student who had just learned the dance, and Brad was with Bonnie, a fifty-something woman who had recently switched from freestyle to ice dance. She had no idea what the counts were, so Brad called out the steps in time to the music. They made it through the dance. So did Monica and Sean, who had been a hockey skater and thus had good edges, uncommon for a beginning ice dancer.

After the Dutch Waltz came the Fourteenstep, which Brad and Monica skated together, to warm up, and then the Kilian. "I've been working on it," Brad said, "So let's give it a try." Monica was surprised at how much deeper his outside edges were, and how much easier the choctaw was to do with him since his lesson on Thursday. Harvey had gotten through to him.

At the end of the 45 minutes, the skaters got off the ice, ready for some coffee or hot chocolate and snacks, which they took turns bringing. Monica grabbed a cup of coffee and a cookie and sat down next to Brad. "So how was the U.P.?" she asked, referring to Michigan's Upper Peninsula.

"Beautiful as always," said Brad, who was from a small town called Hillside, about 30 miles south of Marquette and Lake Superior. "But this was not a pleasure trip."

"What happened?" asked Monica, noticing that Brad had tears in his eyes. She was genuinely concerned.

"My first cousin Don passed away unexpectedly," Brad

began. "He and I were the same age and grew up together. He died suddenly and we were all shocked."

Monica took Brad's hand without thinking and said, "I am so sorry. I had no idea." Brad had only said he was going out of town, not where or why.

Brad put his other hand on top of both of their hands and said, "Thank you." They just sat there together while someone made several announcements that they did not hear. The skaters started to get back on the ice, and Monica gave Brad a big hug.

"Let's skate," he said brightly.

Janet and Julian were walking just behind them. "There's nothing like skating, is there?" Julian said. "No matter what's going on in your life, when you skate, you have to concentrate on what you're doing so much that you just forget everything else." Monica and Brad could not have agreed more.

For the next hour, they skated most of the dances together, except for the golds, which Monica did by herself, to work on strengthening her solo dances, striving for more power and deeper edges. Although she was old enough to pass the adult dance tests, which did not require skaters at least 21 to solo, she wanted to earn the same gold medal that younger skaters earned by doing the dances with a partner, and then soloing. Brad was doing the same thing. They were both strong skaters and Harvey had encouraged their pursuit of these goals. Achieving a gold medal was usually an eight to ten year undertaking for those who stuck with the sport, and they were ahead of the curve.

NOON SKATE

The Zamboni came out to resurface the ice, signaling the end of the Sunday session. Exhausted, Monica and Brad headed for the boards. They were the last ones off the ice and just as Monica was preparing to step through the gate, Brad grabbed her hand and pulled her back. There were no other skaters on the ice. He turned her toward him and planted a sweet, gentle kiss on her lips. Monica thought her knees were going to buckle, but she managed to step off the ice just as the Zamboni driver honked his horn and gave them a thumbs up. The hockey players waiting to get on the ice started clapping and cheering. Monica blushed and wanted to vanish, realizing that what she thought was a private moment had just been shared with an entire hockey team. Surprised and happy with this turn of events, notwithstanding the unexpected audience, she took Brad's hand and they made their way to the lobby.

Chapter Two

T he skaters congregated on the benches where they had left their skate bags and shoes. "I know it's late and you have to work tomorrow, but can I take you out for pizza?" Brad asked Monica. He wasn't ready to let her out of his sight. She quickly agreed and followed him in her car to nearby Julio's, which would be open for another hour.

Monica texted Suzi to let her know she would be late, and she and Brad ordered a medium pizza with pepperoni and sausage. While they were waiting for the pizza, Brad told Monica more about his cousin. "Our families used to raise sled dogs, mostly Siberian huskies, and we had such a great time in the winter with them. My dog, Aliina, that you met last year, is a Siberian husky pup from Don's farm, where he was still living – with his wife and two kids -- when he died. His parents, my aunt and uncle, died years ago."

Monica remembered Aliina from the skaters' Christmas party that Brad hosted last year. The dog was so excited about all the company that Brad almost had to put her in the basement, but she settled down and chewed on a toy in front of the fireplace. Monica remembered how beautiful Brad's house was, located on the side of a hill that overlooked birch and pine trees and snow covered rocks. Floor-to-ceiling windows allowed for a panoramic view of the wonders of nature just outside the glass. Brad, whose great grandparents were Finnish immigrants, told his guests that if they listened carefully, they could hear Finnish spirits whispering in the trees. Maybe one of them was his great grandmother, Aliina, for whom his dog was named.

Great grandmother Aliina had left Finland in 1920, sailing to New York on a passenger ship to find work. She found employment as a maid for a family in Manhattan, where she met Matti Peltonen, Brad's great grandfather. They married and started a life together in Michigan's U.P., where Matti worked in the iron mines and Aliina cooked and did laundry for the miners, many of whom were also Finnish immigrants. When Matti and Aliina heard that free land was available to homesteaders in Hillside, they moved there and built a small farmhouse. Brad's grandfather, Niilo Peltonen, was born there in 1925. Niilo married his high school sweetheart, Miina, from a neighboring farm, and they raised four children, including Don's father, Peter, born in 1947, and Brad's father, Arthur, born in 1950. Arthur married Myra, Brad's mother, whose ancestors had also come from Finland, and they had three children. Brad's younger sisters, Gena and Kaarina, lived in Marquette, not far from their parents in Hillside.

"My cousin Don was buried in the Hillside cemetery, next to his parents and near our grandparents and great grandparents."

Monica knew this was a difficult time for him and just tried to listen. It had been a while since she and Brad had talked about anything other than skating.

"So, enough of that," Brad said. "Tell me about Suzi. Has she decided where to go to college?"

Monica filled him in on Suzi's decision and on her plans to work at the 50-meter pool this summer. They talked until closing time. The waitress gave them a box for the leftover pizza, which Brad suggested Monica take home for Suzi to eat. He left a generous tip and walked Monica out to her car.

"Thanks so much, Brad," she said. "The pizza really hit the spot, and it was nice talking to you."

"Let's do this more often," Brad said, and gave her a hug. They kissed again and drove off - Brad in his dark blue Buick Regal sedan and Monica in her Chevy Cruze. Monica looked forward to noon skate on Monday more than she ever had before. When she got home she checked her phone and found a text from Brad, wishing her a good evening and thanking her for listening. She said it was her pleasure and wished him the same. She added, "Hope I helped."

NOON SKATE

When Monica got to the office Monday morning, she checked a few more cases for Wes, but could not find anything that would help him recover attorneys' fees in Linda Baird's diminished value car case. She put her findings in a brief memo and delivered it to Wes. He said he would talk to Linda and see what she wanted to do. Maybe he could cap his fee at the amount of diminished value, so at least she would not be in the hole if they won the case, which he felt confident about. Monica thought the fee cap sounded like a great idea – she knew Linda did not make a lot of money in her job as a social worker.

Audra and Monica discussed Bob Ritter again and Audra sent out the response to the Office of Special Counsel. "I couldn't talk any sense into Bob," Audra said, shaking her head. "I told him he could cut off his back pay liability by making Ms. Ahmed an unconditional offer of employment, and he did say he would think about it. Now we will just have to wait and see what Ms. Warren wants next."

Monica busied herself with a few new assignments from other attorneys until it was time for noon skate. When she got to the rink, Brad was already on the ice, and so was Callie. They were warming up together, and Callie was smiling from ear to ear. Monica had a moment of doubt, wondering if she had dreamed last night's kisses, but put such thoughts out of her head. She got on the ice, stretched for a few minutes on the boards, and proceeded with five minutes of stroking. Callie started her lesson with Harvey, and Brad joined Monica, taking her hand and stroking with her in unison around the rink.

Janet and Julian approached them while they were standing by the boards catching their breath. "I sent you an email about the spring ice show," Janet said. "We want you two to be in the adult dance number. Harvey will be choreographing it. First practice is next week. Hope you can make it." She skated off.

"Sounds like fun," Monica said. "I wonder what Harvey has in mind." Every year, the Center City Skating Club put on an ice show that featured young skaters as well as adults and usually brought in an up-and-coming champion skater as a headliner. The money raised from ticket sales would benefit the club and help reduce the cost of its sessions, which seemed to go up every year.

"I don't know," Brad said. "But I'm sure Harvey will come up with something fun. He also mentioned a skating competition in Detroit in May. They will be having adult events that we might qualify for, if you are interested."

Monica thought that sounded promising. But right now, she just wanted to skate and get her one hour of ice time in for the day. She and Brad did a pre-silver foxtrot to warm up, and then they put on the music for Brad's Kilian and Blues, which they skated together. Then they split up to work on their individual test dances.

The hour was over before she knew it. Monica gave Brad a hug and went back to work. That night, she and Suzi cooked a meal together. They were eating dessert when Suzi casually mentioned that she had Googled her dad.

"Really?" Monica said, not sure where this was going. She had not thought of Randy in months. "What did you find?"

"Well, he is still in Oregon, running some kind of business. He is also diving again, and his name popped up on a list of masters divers registered for a meet in Ann Arbor in May. Can we go?"

Monica could just imagine what Randy might do if she and Suzi showed up unannounced. She wondered if they would even recognize each other after over 18 years. "Let's think about that," she said. "It might be a good idea for you to email him first, to see how he reacts. Did you find any contact information?"

Suzi said that she had found both an email and a business phone, and would think about what to say in an email to Randy. She would run it by Monica before she sent it. While Suzi was studying, Monica received a call from Brad. She was thrilled -- he was asking her out on an actual dinner date.

"I will make reservations and pick you up on Friday at six. Does that give you enough time?" he asked. Monica put it on her calendar with a big smiley face next to "Dinner – Brad."

Monica reviewed the ice show schedule and added the practices to her calendar. She also looked up the information on the Detroit ice dance competition and learned that there was an Adult Silver Dance event, where both partners must have passed all of their silver dances, but none of their golds. The two competition dances were the European Waltz and the silver Tango. She smiled – she and Brad would clean up in this event, with two of their best dances. She couldn't wait.

She was so excited about her upcoming dinner date with Brad, and the skating events, that she had trouble getting to sleep. When she finally nodded off around 2 a.m., she was awakened by a commotion outside her window. She got up and looked out to find two police cruisers with their red and blue lights flashing. She wondered what had happened but after watching for several minutes, went back to bed.

In the morning, Rose was taking her boys to school when Monica and Suzi were leaving, and Monica asked her if she knew what had happened in the middle of the night. Rose had actually called the manager because she heard a woman screaming in the apartment below hers. She didn't know what happened after that, but the screaming stopped. Maybe the manager had called the police. Monica hoped everything was all right on the first floor. She would ask around later.

That evening, she got home a little early and stopped in the manager's office to ask if she needed to be worried about anything. "I saw the police cars here last night," she said.

The manager, Mr. Cuthbertson, assured her that the police had taken care of it. "A domestic dispute," he said. "No one was injured, but they were very loud. Larisa told me she was trying to break up with the man, so maybe we won't see him anymore."

Monica hoped that was true. Larisa was a young woman from Russia who was trying to make a life for herself in the U.S. She had been married to a U.S. citizen for several years but was now divorced and trying to support her two young children. Monica could empathize with her situation.

*****

Tuesday night was the first ice show practice for the adults. Harvey wanted them to revive the Three-Lobe Waltz, which had been a pre-gold dance many years ago, when he was testing and competing. With eight couples, they could do it as a Rose Pattern, with all of the couples skating on the red circle in the center of the ice and then striking off at the same time to skate circular "petals" of the rose and then coming back into the center circle at the same time. The first time they tried it, there were a few collisions. Callie and her partner Ben, both silver level skaters, had never done the Three-Lobe Waltz and kept getting lost.

"Monica and Brad, would you mind doing it with Callie and Ben this time?" Harvey asked. He could see that Callie and Ben needed stronger, more experienced partners. He put on the music again. This time everything went smoothly. Monica offered to skate with Ben as long as he needed her, and Brad did the same with Callie. Monica wondered if she would get Brad back, but it was not a big deal -- whatever worked for the show, which was coming up quickly in two more weeks.

"What will we be wearing?" asked Monica after practice, hoping she would not have to buy another dress.

Janet suggested that they wear the same red dresses that they used two years ago and add different trim. "And the men can just wear all black. How does that sound?"

The other skaters nodded their agreement. Monica still had her red dress and she knew of a few skaters from two years ago who might want to sell theirs to Callie and Penny, who had not skated in that year's show. They would have only two weeks to come up with a red dress.

On Thursday, Monica partnered Brad through his lesson on the Kilian and Blues, and Harvey asked to see them do the other two pre-golds, the Paso Doble and the Starlight Waltz, which had replaced the Three-Lobe Waltz. Then Harvey let Monica go while he worked with Brad on his solos.

Monica was getting frustrated with the Viennese and Argentine and asked Harvey during her lesson to work with her on the Westminster Waltz, to build on Sunday's group lesson. She wanted to make sure she was practicing the steps correctly and wanted to try doing the dance with Harvey all the way through. Harvey watched her solo, which wasn't too bad. He told Monica to try to take the first lobe of the dance through the center of the rink, where there was a big blue dot. "Your mohawk should go inside the circle, at least." She wasn't getting there on the solo, but when she tried it with Harvey they made it easily and continued on with the rocker-counter section they had practiced on Sunday, and the repeat of the dance, which had a difficult change in partner positions.

"Let's try it with the music," Harvey said, skating over to the boards to put on the "West." They worked up speed on the introductory steps and not only made it inside the circle; they almost reached the blue dot in the very center of the rink for their mohawks. They had just stepped forward from the back edge after the mohawks, when there was a loud crash and someone screamed. Harvey and Monica stopped short and stared at the center of the ice, where they had just been. The large disco ball had fallen from the ceiling of the rink and was laying on its much-dented side, smack dab on the blue dot.

The skaters gathered around the ball, about the size of a large beach ball, but made out of metal covered with thousands of small cut pieces of glass, to reflect colored lights on the popular weekend teen or "disco" skating nights.

"That was close," Brad said, grabbing Monica and giving her a hug. "That could have landed on your head."

"Or mine!" said Harvey. He didn't want to think about what damage the ball could have done to a human skull.

The rink manager came out in his street shoes, slid across the ice and looked at the ball with dismay. "Is everyone all right?" he asked, and when the skaters nodded, he picked up the ball and carried it towards the gate. He came back with a broom and dustpan and swept up the broken pieces of the mirror ball. "No disco skating this week," he said, though they could still have the session for the kids, just not with the added effects of the mirror ball.

Harvey and Monica continued the lesson, a bit shaken even though no harm had come to any of the skaters. Brad kept glancing in their direction, making sure nothing else had happened to Monica.

On Friday at noon skate, Brad confirmed their dinner plans for the evening, and Monica went back to the office. She worked hard to finish her assignments so she could leave at 5 p.m. and get home in time to shower and figure out what to wear.

When Brad arrived at six, he was wearing a light blue sport jacket and navy slacks. Monica was wearing her favorite pink flowered dress and earrings that Suzi had given her for Christmas. "You look stunning!" Brad exclaimed.

"Have a good time," Suzi told them, glad that she would have the car for herself that night. She planned a night out with her girlfriends from the swim team.

"You too," Monica said. "Be safe."

Brad escorted Monica to his car and opened the passenger door of the Regal for her. She couldn't remember the last time someone had done that. She thanked him and settled into the comfortable seat. He drove to the Center City Club, where Monica had never been. They enjoyed a delicious seafood dinner and shared a piece of cheesecake. The conversation flowed easily, from skating to work to past entanglements. Monica wasn't ready to tell Brad all the details of her high school fling that resulted in Suzi, but she did tell him briefly about her short-lived relationships in the last ten years. None of them had lasted more than a year. Suzi had been her priority, especially when she was younger. She asked Brad about Yvonne, a skater he had been involved with for a few years.

"She and I parted ways over a year ago," he said. "We just did not have enough in common, and we wanted different things. She is in the Detroit area now, and we have not kept in touch." Monica knew that Brad had never been married, though Yvonne was not his only ex-girlfriend.

As they were finishing the last bites of cheesecake, they

heard music coming from the end of the room. A band was just starting to play, and Brad asked Monica if she would like to dance.

"Sure," she said, taking his hand. She had never danced with Brad on the dance floor and wondered what kind of dancer he would be. He led her onto the small dance floor and took her into dance position – closer than they would have been on the ice. He led her through a series of foxtrot and swing steps to the big band music that the band was playing. Monica was pleasantly surprised. The band struck up a waltz and Brad drew her in closely for the dance. They whirled around the dance floor and Brad managed to avoid the other couples now swarming onto the floor. Monica was speechless. She had no idea Brad knew how to dance like this.

Brad escorted Monica back to their table and she looked him straight in his brilliant blue eyes and asked, "Where in heaven's name did you learn all of that? You were wonderful!"

He complimented her on her following ability and said, "I have been taking lessons for the last six months – at the Williams Dance Studio. Surprise!"

That was where Monica had taught ballroom dancing for over a year, but that was over ten years ago. Monica couldn't believe it. "Who was your teacher?" she asked.

"Your old friend Margie," he said. "We decided to keep it a secret. I wanted to surprise you one day if I had the chance."

Monica had not spoken to Margie for over a year and

was happy to hear that Margie was still teaching at the studio. She would have to call her and thank her for doing such a good job with Brad.

"I would have taught you for free," she told Brad. "But it's OK. I love surprises." They danced for the rest of the evening. After Brad drove Monica home, they sat in the car and talked for an hour, and then he walked Monica to her door where he kissed her good night. She slipped inside to ice her feet, like she had done in her ballroom teaching days, when her feet ached from hours of dancing. This time she did not mind the pain at all – every dance step had been worth it. Suzi returned a few minutes later and filled Monica in on her girls' night out at a club for teens and young adults.

The next day, Monica called the dance studio and left a message for Margie, asking her to return the call. Suzi was working at the pool and Monica offered to drive her, so she would have the car to do her usual Saturday errands. "Can we grab some breakfast on the way?" Suzi asked.

They got in the Cruze and Monica tried to start it, but the engine would not turn over. She tried several times. "I'm going to be late," Suzi wailed.

Just then Horace from the third floor and a younger man appeared and started to get in a car next to Monica's. "Sounds like a dead battery," Horace said. "Can we give you a jump?"

Horace introduced Monica to his son, Maurice, and proceeded to pull jumper cables out of his vehicle. He attached them to his car and Monica's, and soon her engine was purring.

"You probably need to replace the battery," he said. Monica thanked him and drove Suzi to the pool. Then, instead of grocery shopping, she took the car to the Chevy dealer where she had purchased the car. They were quite busy and it would be a long wait, but she had no choice. She was glad it was the weekend and she was missing neither work nor noon skate.

While Monica was sitting in the customer lounge at the car dealership, Margie texted her, "Lunch today? Terry's Diner on First Street? One o'clock?"

Monica texted Margie that she would try to make it to Terry's if her car was fixed in time. She looked forward to seeing her old friend who had started working at the Williams Dance Studio the same day, over eleven years ago. They were in training class together, and Margie, already an accomplished ballroom dancer, had been very helpful and encouraging. They had a great time teaching together and getting their students through a Pro-Am competition in Detroit and their own local dance Showcase in Center City. Monica remembered that Margie's mom had died just before the Showcase, and it was Margie who had encouraged Monica not to give up on trying to reconnect with her parents in the Detroit area. Monica's parents had disowned her after she became pregnant in her senior year of high school. Thanks to Margie, Monica's efforts finally paid off, and Monica's parents showed up for the Showcase and met their granddaughter for the first time. Since then, they had shared holidays, and Suzi had a relationship with her grandparents.

"You're all set." A man gave Monica a piece of paper and told her to go to the office to pay for her new battery. She took care of it and texted Margie that she was on her way.

The women arrived at Terry's Diner and hugged. "Great to see you!" Margie said. "I was going to call you, but you beat me to it."

They settled into a booth, ordered soup and salad, and started to catch up. "Eric and Becka are running the studio, but Tom still owns it," Margie told Monica. "There are several new instructors, and business is pretty good. I just work three nights a week and have mostly silver and gold level students, but Becka gave me Brad because everyone else was booked."

"That was lucky for him," Monica said. "He led me through foxtrots, swings, waltzes, everything, on Friday. We have been dancing on the ice together for a couple of years but I had no idea he had taken up ballroom dancing."

"He said he wanted to learn the character of the dances, because he had just failed one of them for lack of expression, or something like that."

Monica knew that had been Brad's silver Tango, which he had to retake, and passed the second time with extra points. She had been Brad's test partner. "So, you had something to do with that, too!" Monica exclaimed. "When did you find out Brad and I knew each other?"

"It just came out in the conversation one day. Brad mentioned someone named Monica that he knew from noon skate, and I wondered if it could be you. Recently, he has had a sparkle in his eyes whenever he mentions you. I knew you were going on a date on Friday and wished I could have been a fly on the wall to see how it went. So, tell me all about it!"

"I was very surprised," Monica said. "He is so sweet and kind, and I really enjoy being with him. But it was only our first date."

Their conversation turned to their families, and Monica learned that Margie and her husband Gary were expecting their second child. Their daughter Maria was now eight years old. "We were not planning another one, but he just happened," Margie said. "Maria is excited about having a baby brother."

They finished up their salads and Margie made Monica promise to let her know what happened with Brad. Monica made Margie promise to let her know when the baby came.

Monica finally got around to her errands at the bank and Meijer's Thrifty Acres. Suzi had a ride home from the pool that night, so Monica had the rest of the day to herself. She wondered what Brad was doing but did not want to bother him, knowing that she would be seeing him Sunday night. But she couldn't stop thinking about him.

*****

Brad and Monica arrived at the Sunday adult club session at the same time, put on their skates and enjoyed an evening of camaraderie with the other skaters. During the break, someone announced an ice dance weekend coming up in Washington, D.C. over Memorial Day weekend. This would be three days of ice dancing and socializing with skaters from all over the U.S. and Canada.

Brad said, "That sounds like fun. Any chance you can get away that weekend?"

Monica said she would check her schedule but she didn't know how she could afford the trip. Brad saw the doubtful look on her face and said, "I will cover everything. I really want to do this with you." She promised to look into it and hoped that she could get away from work for a long weekend. She also remembered that Suzi would be going on a trip to New York with a group of seniors from her high school on that weekend – an unofficial senior trip that two of the teachers had put together and would chaperone. So that would be a perfect time for her to get away.

After this invitation, Monica was surprised to see Brad skating with Callie on more dances than he usually did. Monica didn't think much about it and tried to skate with as many of the other men as she could.

On Monday at noon skate, Monica told Brad to go ahead with the D.C. plans. Marcia Day had approved her request for Thursday and Friday of that weekend off, and she was excited about visiting the nation's capital for the first time.

That week, there were two more show rehearsals, which went well. They would have one more the following week, a dress rehearsal and then three shows, on Friday, Saturday and Sunday. Charlotte Walters from Detroit's Motor City Skating Club, who was the national junior ladies champion, would be the guest skater.

Brad called Monica a couple of times during the week

and they talked about everything that was happening. They made dinner plans for Friday and decided to see a movie on Saturday night.

The last show rehearsal went well, and the dress rehearsal did too, but it took forever. Monica's new skates had not come in, so she had no choice but to skate the show in her old skates. She would not need a lot of power on the Three-Lobe Waltz and since she was still skating with Ben, Callie's old partner, she wanted to be sure on her feet in case Ben wasn't. Brad and Callie were having no problems, and Callie seemed to enjoy having a good partner.

The young skaters of the Center City Skating Club put on several group numbers, from little tots to more accomplished high school students. The Center City synchronized skating teams performed their competition programs at various points in the show, with the beginner team going first and the faster and older intermediate team closing the show. The audience enjoyed their formations and seeing so many skaters on the ice at once, all moving together and somehow not crashing. Charlotte Walters amazed the audience with her triple jumps and intricate footwork, and Center City's best young skaters performed well-received individual programs.

The adults skated just after intermission, so they could show up whenever they wanted, as long as they had their skates and costumes on before it was their turn to step onto the ice. All of the women had come up with matching red dresses, and the men, black shirts and pants. On opening night, Monica was pacing around wondering what had happened to Ben. The whole number would be a mess if one couple was missing, and it was too late to add a new skater. Ben was nowhere to be seen and had not responded to calls or texts. Harvey put on his skates and was prepared to skate the number in Ben's place with Monica, which she would not mind at all.

They were all ready to take their spots on the ice, Monica with Harvey, when Ben burst through the door carrying his skates. "I was in an accident on the way here. Am I too late?"

Harvey told him to just relax. "I've got this. Don't worry," Harvey told Ben. "Go have a seat and watch."

The number went well and the audience applauded, including Ben, who was not injured but was understandably upset after being rear-ended by someone on a cell phone. He made it to the next two shows in plenty of time and skated as well as he could with Monica. The adult skaters went out for pizza after the Sunday and last show. There would be no Sunday session that night or again until fall, though the rink would remain open for noon skate and the Center City Skating Club would offer Spring School sessions for its members on week nights.

Monica checked with Barry in the skate shop on Monday. Her new boots and blades had just come in. She tried on the custom-made boots and they felt great, but very stiff, as are all new boots. Barry said he would waterproof the soles to protect her investment and mount the blades with a few trial screws. They would be ready on Tuesday.

"Great!" she said, not looking forward to the two to four

week break-in period that was ahead of her with the new boots, but knowing it was a necessary process if she wanted to skate at gold level.

Monica allowed time on Tuesday to try out the new skates on the ice, to see if the blades were mounted where she wanted them. They seemed fine, so she stroked around in them for several minutes until her ankle bones started to hurt from the stiffness of the boots pressing against them. She switched back to her old skates for the last half of the session. She would return the new skates to Barry so he could put in a few more screws to hold the blades in place.

On Wednesday, she picked up the new skates and paid her balance, trying not to think about the huge dent this would make in her bank account. She put on the new skates and stroked around the rink, trying a few of the easier dances to see how they felt. She switched back to her old skates for her lesson on Thursday, but after three weeks, she no longer had to switch to her old boots. She was able to get more power from every stroke and her ankles no longer hurt after an hour of skating. She was glad she had made the investment.

Brad and Monica worked hard on their test and competition dances with Harvey on noon skate. He gave them new introductions for the competition dances, the European Waltz and the silver Tango, and they worked on creating deeper edges and more flow and expression. Brad was thankful for the ballroom lessons – he now understood what the character of these dances should be. Harvey watched them do the required two patterns of each dance and told them they were looking good and to just stroke out these dances and have fun.

Harvey was also pleased with Brad's progress on the pre-gold Kilian and Blues, and he started working with him more on the Paso Doble, which he thought Brad could have ready, along with the Kilian and Blues, to test on the June test session. He pushed Monica on her Viennese and Argentine, which were getting better and might have a chance of being ready to test in June. They worked on the Westminster Waltz and the Quickstep whenever they had a few extra minutes.

Brad and Monica had been seeing each other every Friday and Saturday for the three weekends since the show. They had attended a play, the Center City symphony, another movie and even a wine festival. And they had gone dancing at the Center City Club a few more times. Monica enjoyed his company both on and off the ice.

At work, Monica learned that Wes had filed a Complaint, or lawsuit, in Linda Baird's diminished value car case, and the other driver's attorney, who worked for her insurance company, had filed an Answer to the complaint. The case was assigned to Judge Anderson in the Center County District Court. They would have three months to complete the discovery process, where each side would serve on the other Interrogatories and Requests for Production of Documents, and take depositions, in an attempt to find out all they could about each other's cases and lock each other into their positions. The trial was set for October. Wes was hoping to settle it before then.

NOON SKATE

In the discrimination case involving their client Bob Ritter, the attorney from the Office of Special Counsel in Washington, D.C., Frances Warren, had called Audra to schedule investigatory on site interviews at Ritter House or Carter Day. She had also requested to see all of the Employment Verification Forms I-9 completed by the company for their new hires in the last two years. Audra and Monica would be present for the interviews of Ritter and his office manager, Janelle Walker, and for the review of I-9 forms. They were trying to decide on a mutually agreeable date in June.

Monica had several other research assignments from other attorneys and had a full plate of work. She looked forward to noon skate every day, when she could get away from the office, get some exercise and see Brad. They always had fun skating together and it was the highlight of her day, as it was for him. If one of them made a mistake, they apologized to each other, sometimes laughing, and continued on. While some partners were constantly arguing about how to do things, Brad and Monica never did. They would discuss the problem and agree to talk to Harvey about it if they couldn't figure it out.

Things were going well, and Monica thought it was time she and Brad talked about deepening their commitment and agreeing not to date others, if there were any. She had no interest in seeing anyone else but wanted to make sure Brad was on the same page. She had made the mistake of not doing this with someone a few years ago and had been shocked when she found out he was dating another woman or maybe two and saw nothing wrong with this. Monica had moved on, vowing to communicate better with the next person she was involved with. That time had come with Brad, she thought. She would talk to him about it this weekend.

NOON SKATE

Chapter Three

Suzi had been in touch with her father, Randy, and he had invited her to watch his springboard diving competition in Ann Arbor in May. Suzi emailed him some photos of herself and Monica and filled him in briefly on what they were doing with their lives and where she was planning on going to college in the fall. Monica agreed to drive down to Ann Arbor with Suzi on Saturday, the second day of the competition, a national masters diving event with over 150 divers competing on one-meter and three-meter springboard, ranging in age from 21 to 90. She mentioned the trip to Ann Arbor to Brad and he seemed supportive.

On the way to the meet, Monica was quite nervous,

wondering how their visit would be. Suzi was also a nervous wreck, about to meet her father for the first time. Monica told her this was normal – and she would be right there if anything did not go well. She hoped Randy would at least be pleasant. They did not have to stay any longer than necessary. Eighteen years was a long time and there would be a lot of catching up to do, but it did not have to be done all in one day. And maybe Randy had other plans. She really had no idea what to expect.

Randy had been the best diver on their high school team. Monica went to every meet with her girlfriends and cheered him on. She thought he was the best-looking boy in the school, with dark brown hair and brown eyes and a slim, muscular build. They didn't have any classes together, but Monica would go out of her way to run into him in the hall between classes and congratulate him on his last diving meet. When he qualified for the state meet, Monica wished him well, and he made the finals. He was planning to dive for a college in Oregon in the fall, where his parents had gone to school.

One day after the state meet, Monica and Randy ran into each other after school and he walked her home. A few days later he asked her to a school dance. They had a good time and he continued to walk her home. They went on several more dates. One thing led to another and Monica found herself pregnant. When she told Randy, he almost fainted. He offered to pay for her to "get rid of it." She couldn't believe it. She looked into all of her options and although she supported a woman's right to choose, it was not her choice to terminate her pregnancy. She kept her situation a secret from her parents and attended her high school graduation ceremony knowing that she was six weeks pregnant. She worked in a restaurant for the summer which was difficult because she kept throwing up every morning. In September, she decided she would have to tell her parents what was going on because classes were starting at the college she was planning to attend and she wondered how she would manage.

When she told her parents, they had the same reaction as Randy and pressured her to end the pregnancy, because she was so young and was planning on going to college in the fall. They didn't want her to "throw her life away" and told her that if she kept her baby, she alone would be responsible for the child and they would not pay for her college education. Moreover, they told her she would need to leave home if she chose to have the baby. Randy went off to college in the fall, but Monica gave up her college dreams for the time being. She thought about running away but had no idea how she would support herself.

Fortunately, Monica found out about a group home called Hannah's House, near Center City, for young pregnant women. She called Hannah's and spoke to Doreen, the housemother, who arranged for Monica to take a bus up to Center City in September. Doreen met her at the bus station. Monica was crying and felt utterly lost and without a friend in the world. Doreen drove her to Hannah's House, a large farmhouse in the country just south of Center City. There, she found five other young women in the same situation, in various months of their pregnancies. They would be allowed to live in the house until their babies were born and could stay up to six months afterward. All of the women were expected to help out with chores and attend classes in the house about caring for babies and parenting.

Hannah's House was supported by private donations and the women did not have to pay anything for room and board. Monica made many friends there and felt that she could not have survived without them. As each baby was born, the others helped out and they were like one big family. Of course, she missed her parents. They had made no effort to contact her even though she had sent them a letter and included the phone number and address of Hannah's House. Whatever happened, Monica knew the other women were there for her and she was in a safe place.

At Hannah's House, Monica learned all she could about caring for infants and was as prepared as any new mother when Suzi was born in February, the year after Monica's high school graduation. Monica was a good mother and she was determined to support herself and the baby. When it came time to leave the home, Doreen helped her find a job and a place to live in Center City. One of the other young women was ready to leave at the same time, and she and Monica shared an apartment for a while. Monica had stayed in Center City ever since, feeling that it was her home.

Monica's thoughts were interrupted as Suzi pulled up the address of the pool in Ann Arbor on her phone and directed Monica to its location on Hoover Street. They found a place to park a few blocks away and walked over to the pool. The diving well was at the far end and they could see divers warming up on the one-meter and three-meter diving boards. Monica and Suzi found seats in the stands, high above the deck, and Monica searched for Randy. The warmup period had just ended and the divers were checking the order that they would dive in, posted on a wall behind the diving boards. They were waiting for the first diver to be announced.

Monica knew from Suzi's research that the divers would be divided into five-year age groups, and Randy would be diving against other men aged 35 to 39 in the one-meter event. The first man got up and did a beautiful forward dive in pike position -- legs straight and toes pointed, while bent at the waist until opening up for a headfirst entry. He made no splash at all. The second diver was Randy! As he got up on the board, Monica's heart skipped a few beats, just as it had in high school when she watched him dive. Randy had gained a few pounds since then and had lost a bit of his curly brown hair, but he was still the best-looking diver on deck. She held her breath while he completed one-and-a-half somersaults in pike position, entering the water cleanly.

There were five divers in Randy's age group, each one doing ten different dives from the three-meter board. Randy received scores of sevens and eights from the five judges, but so did two of the other men. Randy's last dive was a forward one-and-a-half with two twists. He completed the dive, but he was short of vertical and made a big splash. His scores were fives and sixes. When the results were announced, Randy came in second place and was awarded a silver medal. He spotted Monica and Suzi in the stands, put on a pair of warmup pants and a jacket, and made his way up the steps to where they were sitting in the stands.

"Congratulations!" Monica and Suzi exclaimed.

"Thanks for coming," he said. "You look great, Monica. And Suzi – look at you! You look just like your mom did when she was your age. Can you join us for lunch?"

"Us?" asked Monica, just as a woman with a cell phone approached. She had been videotaping Randy's dives and Monica assumed she was another diver.

"This is my wife, Cara," Randy said. "I've told her all about you guys. If you give me a few minutes, I will go and get changed and we can go to Panera down the street." He left Monica and Suzi, who had not known anything of her, to talk to Cara.

"So, how are you?" Monica said awkwardly.

Cara smiled and said she was fine, but more nervous than Randy. "Was he better than this in high school?" she asked Monica.

"Actually, his diving looks about the same as I remember it," Monica said honestly. She glanced down at the deck where much older divers were warming up. "I guess he could keep doing this for years. Looks like they are having fun."

"Randy is enjoying it," Cara said. "He decided to get back in shape this year and this is his first masters meet. The oldest man here is in his 90s, and there are a few women in their 80s. They are amazing."

After what seemed like an hour, but was only fifteen

minutes, Randy appeared and they left the pool for lunch at the Panera Bread restaurant not far away. He asked Suzi all kinds of questions about school, the swim team, work at the pool and her college plans.

Monica asked Randy and Cara how long they had been married and if they had any children. "Five years and yes, we have two. They are back in Oregon with Cara's parents," Randy said.

Suzi couldn't believe Randy had not mentioned this in the emails they had exchanged. "How old are they?" she asked.

"Russell is six and Rita is four," answered Cara. "We would love for you to come see us and meet them some time. They are excited about having a big sister."

Suzi needed to get used to this idea. She had always thought she was an only child, and now, suddenly, she wasn't. She wondered how she would get along with two young siblings. "Sure," she said. "Do you have any pictures of them?" Cara pulled out her phone and shared with Suzi a dozen photos of her children.

"Well, I have to get ready to judge the last diving event today," Randy said. "It was so nice getting together. Let's keep in touch."

Monica doubted that Randy would do this, but Cara seemed nice and she hoped for Suzi's sake that Suzi would have many more visits with her father and his family. As they drove back to Center City, the conversation turned to their respective trips at the end of the month. Suzi was excited about going to New York with her friends. They would be traveling by chartered bus and staying at a youth hostel. They planned to see a Broadway show, visit Ellis Island and the Statue of Liberty, go shopping and do whatever else they could squeeze in. Monica and Brad would be flying from Detroit Metropolitan Airport to Reagan National, across the river from Washington, D.C. They would be staying at a hotel within walking distance of the rink, in Arlington, Virginia, and could take public transportation into D.C. to see the sights, so there was no need for a rental car.

Brad called to find out how the trip to Ann Arbor had gone. "Interesting," Monica said. "I'll tell you all about it tomorrow. Are we still on for the symphony?"

"I'll pick you up at two," Brad said.

The Center City Symphony was performing works by Beethoven and Brahms in the Center City Civic Auditorium in a Sunday afternoon concert. Brad had secured tickets in the sixth row, and Monica enjoyed the music and his company. Afterwards, they went back to his house, took Aliina the husky for a walk and cooked dinner together. After dinner, they enjoyed a glass of wine on the couch by the fire. Monica was trying to figure out how to ask Brad if he thought they should be seeing each other exclusively when he said, "Monica, I am having such a good time with you. These last six weeks have been wonderful and I think I am in love with you."

"I love you, too," she said without hesitation.

Brad assured her that she was the only woman in his life and he could not be happier. They held each other, and

Aliina curled up on the floor next to them. Monica knew that Aliina slept with Brad on his king size bed every night and wondered how the dog would feel about sharing her man in that bed one day.

*****

With only two weeks before the Detroit skating competition, Monica and Brad skated their competition dances, the European Waltz and the Tango, every day at noon skate. Janet and Julian, who were silver level test and competition judges, watched them and gave them some pointers. Janet and Julian were working on their gold level judging appointments, which required trial judging at that level for a prescribed period with a certain level of agreement with the outcome of the tests. They were dedicated to the sport and always willing to be helpful.

One day, Janet observed that Monica and Brad were skating with more expression and told Monica privately, "Whatever you two are doing off the ice, it is helping!"

Monica was a bit embarrassed. She told Janet that she and Brad were in a committed relationship, but that she hoped they had more going than just skating. "I am so afraid that if one of us couldn't skate, our relationship would just fall apart."

"I was afraid of the same thing with Julian," Janet said. "You know, we met on the ice thirty years ago. And we have had a couple of periods of time where one of us was injured or sick and we had to find other things to do together, or we did nothing. But we have been fortunate to always come back to skating. I think if you get along on the ice with a steady partner, you are going to carry that into your relationship off the ice, no matter what you are doing."

Monica felt better and thanked Janet for her advice. In her heart, she knew she and Brad had more than skating, and if for some reason she couldn't skate, she would want him to keep going and reach his goals. She was sure he would want the same for her.

*****

Mother's Day was coming up. Brad asked Monica if he could take her and Suzi out for brunch. Suzi gave Monica a beautiful bouquet of flowers and she and Monica called Monica's mother to wish her a happy Mother's Day. She thanked them for the flowers Monica had ordered. Brad had sent a flower arrangement to his mother in the U.P. and called her before picking up Suzi and Monica. He took them to the Center City Club, which had no music on Mother's Day but offered a sumptuous buffet with all kinds of delicious food. They had fun stuffing themselves and talking about their upcoming skating events, and Suzi's trip to New York.

Brad and Monica had one more lesson with Harvey before the Detroit ice dance competition. "Your dances are looking good," he said. "Have fun and skate well."

Monica's new skates were nicely broken in and she was comfortable skating in them. She planned to wear a gold sequined dress and Brad, a matching shirt – black with gold trim. He picked Monica up in the Regal on Saturday morning, just as Suzi was taking the Cruze to work. "Good luck!" she said, and waved good-bye.

NOON SKATE

The drive down to the Motor City Skating Club took a little over an hour. They were scheduled to skate at 11 a.m. and wanted to get there in plenty of time to change, put their skates on and stretch. They checked in with a monitor at 10 a.m. and she directed them to a clubroom where they could leave their things and put on their skates. They met the other three couples in their event, two from the Motor City Skating Club and one from Lansing. One of the Detroit women was Brad's old girlfriend, Yvonne. Brad got over his surprise and introduced Monica to Yvonne, not sure if Yvonne would remember Monica.

"So, you're still skating?" she asked Brad. "This is my partner, Wally. Nice to see you again, Monica."

They chatted for a few minutes until their group was called out to warm up for two minutes. The music for the European Waltz and the Tango would be played one time each. The four couples took the ice and stroked around the rink, trying to warm up their knees and get the feel of the ice. Brad took Monica's hand as soon as the music came on. They found their starting spot and skated two patterns of the European. Their knees felt good after that and they skated two patterns of the Tango when the music came on. The other couples did the same thing, and no one could really see what the others were doing, since they were all skating. Monica and Brad would compete at the same time as Yvonne and Wally, one couple starting on each side of the rink. Then the other two couples would skate.

The European went well. Brad and Monica tried to remember everything Harvey had told them and had no

69

trouble smiling because they were truly having fun. They thought the Tango went well also. They watched the other two couples in their event and thought they looked good, but possibly not quite as strong. Everyone would just have to wait for the judges to decide the outcome.

While the skaters in the next event warmed up, Monica and Brad and the other three couples stood by the wall where their results would be posted. A woman came along with a piece of paper and taped it to the wall. Brad, who was the tallest, saw the list and held up one finger to indicate to Monica that they had placed first. Yvonne and Wally took second place, and the Lansing couple was third.

Brad gave Monica a hug and they congratulated each other. Yvonne, Wally and the other two couples came over and congratulated them. The medals were awarded a short time later, and Brad and Monica admired the shiny gold medals they had just won. They went out to lunch to celebrate before driving back to Center City. Monica texted Harvey to let him know the results.

The next weekend would be the ice dance weekend in Washington, D.C. and two weeks later, Center City was having its first of three test sessions for the summer. Harvey signed Brad's test application for three pre-gold dances, and Monica's for her gold Viennese Waltz and Argentine Tango. It would be a long day for Harvey, who was partnering his students and those of two female coaches, on over thirty dances. The applications needed to be submitted by a deadline along with test fees for each dance and the signatures of skaters and coaches. This way, the test committee would have plenty of time to arrange for judging panels and food for the judges and volunteers who would be there all day.

*****

On Thursday, Monica took Suzi to school and dropped her off in the parking lot with a backpack and some spending money. She climbed on the chartered bus and found a seat with her friends from the swim team. It would be a long bus ride through Canada to New York. Monica waved and took off for Brad's house where she would leave her car. He drove them to the airport in Detroit and soon they were buckling their seatbelts on the airplane. They checked one bag but carried on their skate bags, which they did not want to take a chance on losing. Monica had just broken in her skates and did not want to go through that again anytime soon, not to mention the cost of replacing them if they were lost. The TSA agents were used to seeing ice skates in the x-ray machines and did not give Monica and Brad any trouble.

The plane landed at Reagan National Airport from the north, giving Monica, in a window seat on the left, a great view of the Washington Monument, the White House, the Jefferson Memorial and the Tidal Basin. The plane banked to the right on approach, and Monica grabbed Brad's hand. She breathed a sigh of relief as the plane landed smoothly. They took their skate bags from the overhead bins and made their way to the terminal.

Brad had reserved a room in the Crystal City Aurora Hotel, just a block away from the rink where the ice dance weekend, hosted by the Crystal City Skating Club, would be held. They took a taxi to the hotel with their skate bags and luggage, checked in and went for a walk. They figured out how to get to the rink and came across the Crystal City metro stop, so they went in, bought fare cards and consulted a map.

"We have all afternoon," Brad said. "Let's go to D.C. and see the sights." He had been to Washington before but it had been a while. They saw an ad for the D.C. Duck tours, in an amphibious vehicle that would take them everywhere they wanted to go. They took metro to Union Station and bought tickets for the next Duck tour. Soon they were on the Duck, being whisked all over the Capitol area, to the White House, the monuments and into the Potomac River. Monica took pictures and emailed a few of them to Suzi, hoping she would do the same. She got back a photo of the kids sleeping on the bus, half way to New York.

After the tour, Brad and Monica enjoyed a delicious dinner at one of the restaurants in Union Station and looked around at the many shops. Monica picked out a t-shirt for Suzi with cherry blossoms on it, apparently left over from the Cherry Blossom festival.

On Friday, Brad and Monica took metro into D.C. again and visited several Smithsonian museums, which they could not believe were completely free to the public. They had lunch at the National Museum of the American Indian, which offered food from Native American cultures. Brad was starting to worry that he had not heard from his next-door neighbor, Richard, who was taking care of Aliina, but while they were eating lunch, he received a text that his husky was doing just fine. Richard added, "She sure has a lot of energy."

The dance weekend began with a two-hour programmed dance session on Friday night. When they checked in at the rink, the women were given a blue ribbon or a red ribbon to indicate what flight they would be allowed to skate of each dance on the program. Since there were twice as many women registered for the event, the men would have to do double duty, skating both flights, the first with a "blue" woman and the second with a "red" woman. Monica was red. She and Brad agreed to do all of the pre-gold dances together on the red flight, so Brad would have a chance to skate with his test partner. Monica wondered if any of the men would ask her to skate. Of course, women were free to ask the men, too.

There were skaters from all over the U.S. and Canada. Most of them knew most of the dances, even if they were skating them "socially" and not at the test level of the higher dances. The session started with the Swing Dance, a preliminary level dance that was easy to do with a stranger. Brad skated the first flight with a woman from Texas and grabbed Monica for the next flight, so the other men could see what she could do. He also skated her flights of the next two dances, the Fourteenstep and the European Waltz, with her. By then, the other men had noticed Monica and she did not have to sit out a single dance. Brad would have skated all of her dances with her, but sometimes women asked him to skate before he could get to Monica. He also knew the idea of the dance weekend was more social, and it was fun to skate with other people, even though he had his one favorite partner. The men were exhausted when the Zamboni appeared, and Brad wondered how he would get through two more days of skating double flights.

The skaters helped themselves to snacks provided by the Crystal City Skating Club and mingled with their fellow ice dancers, comparing notes on their coaches and home ice dancing sessions. The second hour included a Paul Jones mixer, where the men were directed to form a circle and the women, another circle outside of the men's circle. The circles would move in opposite directions and when the music stopped, the skaters would pair up with whoever was in front of them for the Dutch Waltz or another preliminary dance that everyone would know. After the session, the skaters enjoyed wine and cheese in a clubroom overlooking the rink.

Monica and Brad slept well after all of the exercise and headed back to the rink in the morning after breakfast in the hotel. Three well-known local coaches were conducting a clinic, offering group instruction on three different levels of dance and on power stroking. Brad and Monica joined the pre-gold and gold group and picked up some pointers on partnering the Quickstep, a gold dance that Monica had just started working on with Harvey. A buffet lunch was served after the clinic, and then there were two more hours of programmed ice dancing. Monica and Brad skated with many other partners but found each other again for pre-golds and their recent competition dances, the European Waltz and the Tango.

Saturday evening, the skaters attended a dinner dance in the host hotel. Monica wore a light blue tea length dress with matching earrings and silver dance shoes. Brad wore a dark blue coat and tie. After a delicious buffet, they danced to the music of a small band from Arlington. Many of the ice dancers had taken ballroom dancing lessons, so there were plenty of couples crowding the small dance floor on every dance. Brad led Monica through tangos, waltzes, foxtrots, cha chas and many more dances, weaving in and out of the crowd. They managed not to run into anyone. They had fun but missed the much more spacious floor at the Center City Club.

The Crystal City Skating Club provided a nice Sunday morning breakfast buffet at the rink, before one last two-hour programmed dance session. Some of the skaters had already gone home, and a few more of the local men showed up, so the group was smaller and the women were not flighted – they could skate either or both flights of any dance. Monica and Brad skated both flights of every pre-gold dance, and she told him that the dances were really feeling good. One of the local coaches who had taught the Saturday clinic asked Monica to do the Viennese Waltz, Argentine Tango and Westminster Waltz, which thrilled her. She was able to keep up with him, thanks to her new skates and all the work she had done on these dances with Harvey. The Sunday session ended with the Grand March: one of the Crystal City men directed everyone as they skated down the ice, first in two single lines, then in pairs, groups of four, etc. The skaters joined hands and the leader wound everyone around in ever-tightening circles and back out to where they came from. Monica was the last person on the chain and got whipped around, almost crashing into the boards, but she held on. After a few more moves of the Grand March, everyone got off the ice, said their goodbyes and headed home, worn out from all of the skating and dancing.

Monica spent Sunday night with Brad and Aliina, who jumped for joy when they arrived. They took the dog for a long walk in the neighborhood and stopped by the neighbor's house to thank him. The next day was a holiday, so Monica could sleep in and spend the day with Brad. They had a leisurely breakfast, took Aliina out and watched a movie on Brad's big screen TV. When Monica got a text from Suzi that her bus was almost back from New York, she gave Brad a big hug and kiss, thanked him again for a wonderful weekend, and headed to the high school to pick up her daughter.

Suzi emerged from the bus rubbing her eyes. She climbed in the Cruze with her backpack and a shopping bag from Macy's. Monica knew better than to ask her about the trip – the details would come out eventually. She drove home where they could both sleep in their own beds and hopefully get a good night's sleep.

*****

When Monica got back to the office on Tuesday, she learned that Ms. Warren, the Office of Special Counsel attorney, would be coming to Center City the following week. Audra and Ms. Warren agreed to meet at Carter Day, and Bob Ritter and Janelle Walker would come there with the I-9 forms that Ms. Warren had requested. Audra thought it better not to meet at Ritter House because Ms. Warren might think of something else she wanted to see there. Monica thought it was funny that she had just been to Washington, D.C. and now someone from there was coming to Center City.

Linda Baird's deposition and the depositions of the experts on diminished value were set for the week after that. Wes asked Monica to sit in. "Strength in numbers," was the reason he gave, but he also realized that Monica knew the case and might have some ideas if he forgot anything.

*****

With the test session just two weeks away, Monica and Brad skated pattern after pattern of their test dances. Harvey gave them some extra lesson time, which helped to ease their nerves. Monica was still collapsing out of her twizzle sometimes, so she practiced dozens of them at the end of the rink. She and Brad were not the only ones testing, and tempers were running short. Callie accused another skater of cutting her off – not giving her the right of way. Monica had to keep stopping on the Viennese when others got in her way, and she had to fight the urge to yell at them. When the weekend came, Monica and Brad went to the Center City Club to try to get their minds off the test session. They enjoyed an hour of ballroom dancing and felt a lot better.

On Tuesday, the day Ms. Warren would be coming to Carter Day, Monica had to be at the office early to meet with Audra, Bob Ritter and Janelle Walker. Suzi would get a ride to school later with a friend. But when Monica went out to her car, she found, to her dismay, that the left front tire was flat. She was fumbling in her purse for her phone and the number of her insurance company, so they could arrange for a tow truck, when Horace came out of the building.

"I can help with that," he said. Monica didn't want him to be late for wherever he was going and said she would call for help, but Horace insisted. "What are neighbors for?" he said, proceeding to pull a jack out of his car and the spare tire out of Monica's trunk.

Twenty minutes later, Monica was driving off, thanking Horace for his help. He was such a good neighbor. She wondered what she could do for him in return.

Monica arrived at the office just as Bob Ritter and Janelle Walker were getting out of their cars. They walked in together and Monica showed them to Audra's office. She went to her office to pick up a few things and returned as Audra was telling them that it was important for them to answer Ms. Warren's questions and to tell the truth, but they need not volunteer information. They said they understood.

Anna, the receptionist, buzzed Audra to let her know Ms. Warren had arrived. A conference room had been reserved for the interviews, and Audra asked Anna to take Ms. Warren there. Soon, everyone was gathered at the large conference table.

Ms. Warren thanked Ritter and Ms. Walker for coming in and said, "This is going to be very informal. I will just need to ask you some questions about your business. Mr. Ritter, how long have you been in business?"

NOON SKATE

Bob Ritter talked about his twenty years in business in Center City, where he operated three furniture stores, employing over one hundred employees. Ms. Warren then asked Ms. Walker to describe the hiring process at Ritter House.

"They come in, sometimes with a resume, and fill out an employment application. I review the application, interview the person and then consult with Mr. Ritter. Then we check references. If the person is hired, we would have them fill out an I-9 form and tax form. Then we would put them on the schedule." Monica thought that Ms. Walker must have changed her procedures a bit, because she had told Monica that she had completed Ms. Ahmed's I-9 form right after the interview, but Monica could not say anything. Audra had reminded her that anything Bob Ritter and Janelle Walker told her was privileged.

Ms. Warren asked Ms. Walker to tell her what happened with Sarah Ahmed, who had filed the charge of discrimination against Ritter House. "Well, she seemed like a good candidate," Ms. Walker began. "You can see from her resume she has lots of experience. She interviewed well and I told her we would get back to her. Then a more qualified candidate came along, and we hired her instead. I'm sure Ms. Ahmed must be disappointed, but we did not discriminate."

Monica was trying not to let her jaw drop. Ms. Walker was lying through her teeth. She had admitted to Monica that she had not hired Ms. Ahmed because Mr. Ritter did not want to hire anyone who wasn't born in the U.S. or who looked like a terrorist. But Monica could say nothing.

Ms. Warren pulled out the I-9 form completed by Ms. Ahmed and signed by Ms. Walker on behalf of Ritter House. She asked Ms. Walker if that was her signature, and Ms. Walker said yes.

"So, in this instance, you completed the I-9 form on the day of the interview?" asked Ms. Warren.

"Uh, yes," Ms. Walker said.

"So you knew Ms. Ahmed was not a U.S. citizen, right?" asked Ms. Warren.

"Yes."

"Did that have anything to do with the decision not to hire Ms. Ahmed?"

Ritter and Ms. Walker shook their heads. "No," Ritter declared. Monica wondered what Audra was thinking. Her clients were lying to the government attorney.

Ms. Warren then asked to see the I-9 forms she had requested, and Ms. Walker handed her the file. While she was reviewing the forms, Audra asked Ritter and Ms. Walker to step outside with her and Monica. They closed the door to the conference room and went to Audra's office.

"Mr. Ritter, do you realize you have an obligation to tell the truth to the government? I strongly recommend that you tell Ms. Warren the truth and let the chips fall where they may."

Bob Ritter sat down and put his head in his hands. "What if we just give her some money to go away?" he asked. "How much does Ms. Ahmed want?"

Audra said she would find out and went back to the

conference room, where she had a discussion with Ms. Warren about resolving the case. Ms. Warren said she would talk to Ms. Ahmed and get back to Audra regarding the amount of back pay that Ms. Ahmed would be entitled to and the amount of a civil penalty that Mr. Ritter would be asked to pay. Both attorneys hoped they could work out a written settlement agreement that would be acceptable to both sides. Ms. Warren finished reviewing the I-9 forms and left the office. Monica was relieved when Audra came back and told them that she thought the matter could be resolved.

"We will wait to see how much money is involved and I will be in touch with you," Audra told her client. He and Ms. Walker headed for the door.

By that time, it was almost noon. Monica couldn't wait to get to noon skate and see Brad. They wanted to skate as many patterns of their test dances as possible to get ready for the test session on Saturday.

On Thursday, they had their last lesson with Harvey before the tests. First, Harvey watched Brad and Monica skate Brad's three pre-gold dances together. Then he watched Brad's solos while Monica practiced her gold dances by herself. On her lesson, she skated the Viennese Waltz and Argentine Tango well with Harvey and felt good on her solos – even the twizzles on the Argentine. Harvey gave her some positive comments but looking at her skates, he said, "Those are covered with black marks. Give them a good coat of polish before Saturday."

Monica had scuffed up the insides of both boots from bringing her feet together as she was supposed to, and the toes of both boots were peppered with small holes from men who had kicked her with their toe picks during the ice dancing sessions in Washington. She went to the skate shop at the Center City Ice Arena on Friday and purchased a small bottle of white shoe polish. She saw the test schedule posted on a bulletin board near the rink and took a picture of it with her phone to send to Brad. The tests would start at 9 a.m. on Saturday with preliminary dance tests and work up to golds by the end of the day at 4 p.m. Brad and the other pre-gold testers would start at 1 p.m., so Monica told Brad she would see him at the rink at noon, to give them plenty of time.

When she got home after work, Monica took her skates inside and gave them a coat of white polish. She left them to dry on the coffee table and made dinner. She and Suzi enjoyed a meal of pork chops and a green bean casserole. Suzi was looking forward to her senior prom on Saturday and had purchased a beautiful light yellow dress. Her longtime friend Miles had asked her to prom, and would pick her up in his parents' Buick. Monica said she would be back from the test session in plenty of time to help Suzi get ready.

After dinner, a friend picked Suzi up to go out for a few hours, and Monica read a book to try to relax and get her mind off the test session. She had tested many ice dances but still got nervous, thinking of all the things that could go wrong. Suzi returned at 11:30 and after a snack, she and Monica went to bed. Monica fell into a fitful sleep.

At 2 a.m., Monica woke up to a shrill noise which she

quickly realized was the smoke detector going off. The smoke detector was mounted on the wall between Suzi's bedroom, closest to the living room, and Monica's room just down the hall. Monica jumped out of bed and started to open the door but realized smoke was pouring underneath the door into her bedroom and the door felt hot.

"Suzi!" she screamed. "Get up!" There was no answer. More smoke was coming under the door. She dared not open it, fearing that there were flames on the other side and kept screaming for Suzi to wake up. She stuffed the contents of her dirty clothesbasket under the bedroom door to try to block the smoke.

Glancing in the direction of her bedroom window, Monica saw flashing red lights coming from the parking lot and threw open the curtains to find several fire trucks outside. She could see flames coming from the windows below. She opened the window, kicked out the screen and yelled, "Help me, please! My daughter is trapped! Help!"

As the smoke grew even thicker, Monica leaned out the window and could see a fireman on a ladder trying to reach her. She dug her feet into a nearby pair of old sneakers, grabbed her purse and cell phone, which she always kept on the night stand near her bed, and extended her hands to the fireman. "My daughter," she gasped. "Next window!"

Another ladder was already being extended up to Suzi's window. The fireman kicked in the screen, broke the window, and disappeared inside. Moments later, he emerged with Suzi in his arms and handed her to another fireman on the ladder. Monica, still gasping for breath, was waiting for them at the bottom of the ladder. Suzi was taken to an area where several ambulances were waiting. Monica's car was blocked by all the fire trucks so she climbed into the ambulance with Suzi and the EMTs.

As the ambulance pulled out of the parking lot, Monica was horrified to see the entire apartment building engulfed in flames. Fire trucks were all over and firemen were trying to rescue residents from the second and third floors. She prayed that they would all get out safely. The ambulance was half way to the hospital when she remembered her skates - nicely broken in and freshly polished – on the coffee table.

"What is it?" the EMT asked her.

"My skates are in the building," she moaned. The EMT rolled his eyes, probably thinking of cheap skates from Sears, and not ones that had cost Monica more than an entire paycheck.

Monica knew that skates could be replaced but she tried not to think about how much that would cost her, whether insurance would cover it, and how long it would take to get a new pair and break them in all over again. She told herself that there would always be another test session. Right now, her biggest concern was her daughter. Suzi was being given oxygen, and the EMT said she was going to be fine, but she needed to go to the hospital. Monica did not quarrel and hoped he was right about the outcome. It could have been much worse, she thought – at least Suzi did not appear to be burned. But she had been closer to the fire and might have inhaled more smoke than Monica.

NOON SKATE

Other ambulances were arriving with victims of the Southside Apartments fire, and emergency room personnel were doing their best to take care of everyone. Monica sat in a waiting room while Suzi was examined and treated. She called Brad to tell him where she was and what had happened. She was so distraught that she was not making a lot of sense, but Brad gathered that he needed to come to the hospital right away.

Brad got there in fifteen minutes, wearing an old pair of warmup pants and a sweatshirt. He found Monica wearing her sweats and old sneakers and took her into his arms. She smelled like smoke, and tears were streaming down her face.

"It was the worst thing I have ever seen," she said. "If the smoke detector had not gone off, I don't know if we would have made it out of there." She started to worry about Rose and her boys, about Horace, and about the Singh family on the third floor. She prayed that they were all right.

"My skates were in the building," Monica said. "I guess that means I won't be skating tomorrow – er, today. And Suzi's prom dress is in there."

"For heaven's sake," Brad said. "The only thing that matters here is that you and Suzi are safe. I'm sure they will let us test on the next session. I will call the test chairperson and let her know what has happened."

Monica was thankful to have Brad there. They sat together waiting for someone to tell them how Suzi was doing. Monica didn't know what she would do if anything happened to her only child, a girl who was supposed to have her whole life ahead of her.

Chapter Four

After what seemed like hours, a doctor appeared and told Monica that Suzi was still on oxygen and he wanted to keep her in the hospital for at least 24 hours for observation. He told Monica to go home and get some rest.

"Home?" she said, starting to cry. "It's all gone. Everything is gone. The fire destroyed it all."

"I'm so sorry," said the doctor, as Brad put his arm around Monica.

"You can come home with me," Brad said. "I will bring you back after we get some rest."

Monica signed some papers, looked in on Suzi, and told her she would be back later in the morning. Suzi was awake and alert, but coughing and having trouble speaking. Monica told her there had been a fire but they got out, thanks to the fire department, and she was going to be fine. Suzi nodded, looking terrified, but motioned for Monica to leave.

Brad and Monica arrived at his house where Aliina sniffed Monica's smoky clothing. "Can I borrow a shirt or something?' Monica asked, and Brad gave her a pair of pants, a shirt, and a pair of his pajamas.

Monica took a shower and changed into Brad's very large pajamas. She fell asleep for a few hours in his guest room and woke to find Aliina sitting on her face. "Blaaah!" she sputtered, giving the dog a gentle push. Brad was just coming in with a tray of cereal, hard-boiled eggs and coffee. He turned on the TV in the room and sat down on the bed with Monica.

The local TV news was reporting on the Southside Apartments fire. They were showing video footage of the blaze, which had been a seven-alarm fire. Twelve fire engines and six ladder trucks – almost the complete Center City fleet - had sped to the building. The Center City Fire Chief said in an interview that they suspected arson, and that an accelerant must have been used, because the fire was so intense and spread so quickly. He also stated that the fire doors may have been propped open. Their investigation over the next few weeks would determine the exact cause. He emphasized the need for working smoke detectors, which many residents probably did not have, or if they did, they might not have changed the batteries. If they had even a minute's warning from a smoke detector, they might have escaped sooner without injuries.

Monica told Brad that was what she thought had saved them – the smoke alarm had given her just enough time to get out before the fire reached the bedrooms.

The TV newscast switched to the hospital, where a representative told the reporter that over fifty people had been admitted for treatment of smoke inhalation and burns. No one taken to the hospital had succumbed to their injuries, but there was no way to know yet if anyone had died in the apartment building, unable to escape the fire.

The news reporter added that the building was a complete loss. The fire department had first tried to rescue as many residents as possible with ladders from the second and third floors before turning hoses on the burning building, which they had no hope of saving and were still trying to extinguish. Those residents not taken to the hospital had gathered in the park next door and were given shelter in a nearby church if they had nowhere to go. The Red Cross was supplying food and clothing to the survivors, and the church was asking for more donations.

Monica felt fortunate to have Brad, and he was thankful he was there to help her. "You and Suzi can stay here as long as you need to," he said. He had been hoping that things would work out so that he and Monica would have a future together, but he had not expected them to be living together this soon, and not for this reason. He would save the topic of a more permanent life together to discuss with her another time, when they were over this crisis.

After breakfast, Brad took Monica back to the hospital.

NOON SKATE

She sat in Suzi's room while she slept, and made a list of things she would need to do to try to get back on her feet. First, she would need to call the insurance company. She had renter's insurance with a $500 deductible, which meant she would have to pay the first $500 to cover the cost of her new pair of skating boots and blades, which would cost well over $1,000. In addition, she had lost all of her furniture, clothing, and personal items, which would be covered, but she wondered how long it would take to get reimbursed for the loss. The insurance company was going to think she was a magnet for trouble – first the flood and now a fire. She hoped her insurance would not be cancelled. She wondered if her car had been damaged with all the fire trucks coming and going. Then, thinking of the car, she tried to recall what she had done with her old broken-down skates. Were they still in the trunk? She could not remember what she had done with them. If they were in the trunk of her car, then she could at least skate in them for a few weeks while she was waiting for new skates. She had not thought about the old skates for weeks and had been planning to donate them to a used skate sale that the synchronized skating teams were having.

Her thoughts were interrupted when a doctor came in to examine Suzi. "You are doing well, young lady," the doctor said. "You can probably go home tomorrow."

"What about the prom? It's tonight!" Suzi said. "And where is my phone? I need to call Miles."

The doctor indicated that the prom was not a possibility, but told her she might be able to go to school on Monday.

He didn't get the response from Suzi that he was looking for, which was understandable. He said there was a danger from infection in the lungs, because of the smoke inhalation, and Monica would have to watch Suzi closely.

Monica told Suzi that she and Brad were going to drive over to Southside and see what was left, and if they found her phone, they would bring it to her, but Monica didn't think there was much chance of that. She gave her phone to Suzi to call Miles and tell him she would be missing the prom.

Even though she had seen the video footage on TV, Monica was completely unprepared for what she saw when she and Brad pulled into the parking lot of Southside Apartments. Several fire trucks were still there trying to douse the smoldering remains of what had once been Monica's home. There was no chance of getting anywhere near the building or of finding any belongings at all. Somewhere in all that rubble was a pair of very expensive skates but even if the steel blades had survived the inferno, there was no way to find them. She was relieved that her car was still where she had parked it, though it was now covered with soot.

Monica ran to her car and opened the trunk. In the back, she saw her old skates and grabbed them. There were a few sweaters and other odds and ends, but no change of clothes. Monica was still in Brad's shirt and pants and her old sneakers. She told Brad she would need to stop by Meijer's on the way back to the hospital and pick up some socks, underwear, a couple of pairs of jeans and shorts for herself, and a few changes of clothes for Suzi. But before they could go anywhere, Rose pulled up and got out of her car. She saw Monica and gave her a big hug. Tears streamed down both women's faces.

"I'm so glad you made it!" Monica said. "How are the boys?"

"We had to jump out the window," Rose said. "The Singhs had just been rescued from the third floor and they had a blanket with them, or maybe they got it from the fire department. They and two other neighbors held the blanket by all four corners and I told Ricky to jump. He was terrified, but he jumped. Then Tommy had to go. The fire was getting closer and I was afraid he wouldn't go, so I gave him a push. He screamed but he landed on the blanket and they are both fine. They are with their grandma. How is Suzi?"

"She's in the hospital but will hopefully be released tomorrow. We're staying with Brad." She introduced Brad to Rose, and he said he was glad her family survived such a horrendous night. He truly felt sorry for everyone involved.

"Have you heard who might have set the fire?" Rose asked. "I saw Larisa in the park after we jumped. She had climbed out of her first-floor window unharmed, as did most of the people on the first floor. Larisa told me that her ex-boyfriend, the one that she was fighting with that time, had been over again and threatened to kill her. She called the police and they told her to get a protective order. She thinks he came back and set the fire."

"How could anyone do such a thing?" Monica said. She

hoped Rose and Larisa were mistaken.

Rose had come to see what was going on, and other residents, or former residents, were doing the same thing. They stood in small groups, trying to console each other. "At least we have our lives," many were saying, and then the next moment, "We lost everything!"

Monica noticed Horace's son Maurice with a woman and a baby. She approached them and asked Maurice how his father was.

Maurice stared at the burning rubble and said, "I haven't heard from my father. I called the hospital and they do not have anyone there who fits his description. He was not one of the people who were in the park, and the police have no idea where he is. The firemen told me that they can't search for bodies until the fire is put out." He started to cry.

"I hope he is alive somewhere," Monica said, hoping Horace had jumped or was rescued and just did not have access to a phone.

Maurice introduced Monica to his wife Bonita and their infant son, Anthony. Bonita said she hoped they found Horace soon because she wanted her son to have a grandfather.

Monica and Rose hugged again and exchanged numbers so they could keep in touch. They had never needed each other's phone numbers before – they just went across the hall if they wanted to talk or borrow something. She would miss Rose and her two boys and wished them well, wherever they ended up. Rose was lucky to have a good job as a nurse and could stay with her mother for a while.

NOON SKATE

Brad went off to do some errands and Monica went to Meijer's to buy clothing and other personal items – shampoo, hairbrushes, toothpaste, dental floss, and deodorant. The list seemed endless, but she tried to limit her purchases for now, not knowing what the insurance company was going to do. She called them from her car in Meijer's parking lot, finally having a few moments to herself.

"Um, I just lost everything except my car and my life in a fire," Monica said. The claims representative said she was very sorry to hear that and directed Monica to the company's website where she could complete a list of everything that had been destroyed and what its replacement value would be. "Once we have reviewed the information, we will issue you a check."

"How long will that take?" asked Monica.

"Probably two weeks. I will try to expedite it for you. Do you have a place to stay?"

Monica said she did, but she wasn't sure for how long. Brad had plenty of room, but she wasn't sure how comfortable Suzi would be there. She thought they would be able to get through the summer – until Suzi went off to college in September. Then she would figure out what to do. She hoped she had a future with Brad, but she did not want to take anything for granted. If he didn't think so, then the sooner she moved out, the better.

Spotting a car wash across the street, Monica drove her soot-covered car over and paid for a much-needed wash. The Cruze glistened afterwards. While Monica was waiting, she got a text from Margie, her friend and former co-worker at the Williams Dance Studio, asking if she was OK. Monica wrote her a quick reply saying she was fine and would tell her more later. She sent the text and drove back to the hospital.

Brad stopped by the ice dance test session at Center City Ice Arena to let everyone know that Monica and Suzi were safe. Harvey was on the ice with one of his young skaters and could not talk. The test chairperson, Ruby Anderson, told Brad not to worry, that she had already set them up on the next test session for no extra money. Everyone told Brad to wish Monica well and that they hoped she would be back on the ice soon.

"She will be," Brad said, "But her new skates went up in flames so she will need to order new ones. She will be skating in her old skates for a while."

Janet and Julian expressed dismay at the fate of the new skates. "And she had just broken them in," Janet said. "That is awful! I would not want to break in another pair so soon. Her poor feet! But we are glad she's OK."

When Monica arrived at Suzi's hospital room, one of the doctors was with her. He said, "We are going to let her out of here, but not until tomorrow morning. She will need to see her family doctor in a week to make sure there are no signs of infection. Some people develop pneumonia after smoke inhalation, so if she has any trouble breathing, call us right away."

Monica thanked the doctor and stayed to visit with Suzi for a while. She said she had been in touch with Miles and that he was very understanding about the prom. He offered to take her out to dinner in a few weeks when things had settled down. When she got to Brad's house, she found that he had prepared a lovely dinner of steak and mushrooms with a tossed salad. Monica realized she had not eaten since breakfast and was thankful for Brad's consideration. There was no way she had the energy to prepare a meal that day. She enjoyed the dinner, a big glass of red wine, and Brad's company.

After a quiet evening, they retired to Brad's king size bed. Suddenly, Monica sat up and said, "Do you have a smoke detector in here?"

"Yes, of course," Brad said. "It's right out there in the hall. And we also have Aliina. She would wake us if anything is wrong."

"When did you change the batteries?" Monica asked, trying not to sound paranoid, but she had almost died in a fire and was not about to leave anything to chance.

"Just a month ago. Trust me, the smoke detector is in working order and you have nothing to worry about." He pulled Monica close and wished he could take away her anxiety. He didn't know it, but he already had. They fell asleep in each other's arms, with Aliina at their feet.

Early Sunday morning, Monica got to the hospital and gave Suzi a bag from Meijer's with the newly purchased clothing to tide her over. "You can change into something else that I picked up yesterday, and we can go shopping for more things later, including a new phone. Yours will not be recovered."

Suzi looked in the bag and changed into a pair of jeans that Monica had picked out, a Hello Kitty t-shirt and pink flip-flops. "Can I see the fire?" she asked.

Monica wondered whether that would be a good idea but decided to drive over to Southside so that Suzi could start to let it all sink in – that she had lost everything and would be starting over, but she was alive. Monica parked across the street and Suzi just stared at the rubble. She said nothing. "Where are we going to live?" she finally asked. "And how will I study for final exams if my books and notes are gone?"

"Maybe you can borrow some books and get the notes from someone." Monica hoped the high school would understand – Suzi was probably not the only student in this situation.

They stopped at Meijer's again so Suzi could pick up a cheap smart phone and get reconnected with her friends, if she could remember their numbers, or she would get on Facebook and find everyone there. Then they went to Brad's house. Brad showed Suzi the guest room, with a freshly made up double bed and a set of towels. Monica would have to bunk in discreetly with Brad and Aliina.

The Sunday morning newspaper arrived; the Southside fire was still front-page news. A photo showed firemen trying to douse the last of the glowing embers. There was a detailed account of everything that was known at that point. Monica and Brad read it together. They learned that two men had been arrested, Larry and Douglas Howard, of Center City. A surveillance camera at a business across the street had picked up two men carrying gasoline cans into Southside Apartments at 2 a.m. Saturday morning. They exited the building hastily five minutes later and in seconds, flames could be seen on the first floor. The Fire Chief surmised that the men had gone in the building, opened all the fire doors, poured gasoline down the hallways and lit a match as they were leaving the building. A police officer who had dealt with Larisa's complaints about her ex-boyfriend recognized one of the men as the ex-boyfriend, Larry Howard. Larry was picked up Saturday night and implicated his brother, Douglas, as his accomplice. Both men were being held in the county jail without bond, charged with arson and first-degree murder.

"Murder?" Monica was afraid to keep reading. That meant that someone died in the fire. The newspaper reported that the remains of one person had been found and that his or her identity was being confirmed with dental records. She prayed that it wasn't Horace.

Suzi asked to go to the mall to get some clothes for school, and Monica needed some for work, as well as warmup pants and a jacket for skating. And they both needed shoes, so they headed for the Center City Mall. There, they ran into Rose and her boys, who were doing the same thing – trying to start over. Monica found a black skirt, jacket and pants, and several blouses that she could mix and match, and Suzi picked out two new outfits. They both found sneakers and work or school shoes at Payless.

Suzi ran into Candice, a girl from her school who had lived at Southside. "Are you starting over, too?" Suzi asked.

"Yes," the girl said. "My mom gave me fifty bucks -- that will have to stretch a long way. Is your family OK?"

Suzi told Candice that she had been in the hospital but she was fine, and so was her mother. "See you in school."

Brad took Monica and Suzi to a movie that afternoon, and they went out for pizza afterwards. They dropped Suzi off at a friend's house for the evening and went back to Brad's to watch another movie on his big screen TV – something light and funny with no fire in it. Suzi got a ride home and came in just as the movie was ending.

Brad took Aliina out for her nightly business while Monica and Suzi got ready for bed. After he and the dog returned and Suzi said good night, Aliina followed her into the guest room. Suzi and Brad looked at each other.

"Do you mind her?" Brad asked Suzi. "If she bothers you, just shoo her out and close the door."

"She's fine," Suzi said, wondering what Aliina was going to do. Suzi climbed into bed and Aliina jumped up with her and lay down next to her. Suzi stroked the dog's head and said, "Want to sleep with me, girl?"

Aliina made a strange gurgling noise and put her head down, as if to say, "Time for bed. I'm here for you."

In the morning, when Monica went into the guest room to make sure Suzi was awake, she found Aliina curled up with Suzi, one of Suzi's arms around the dog. It was the sweetest thing she had ever seen. Somehow, Aliina knew where she was most needed and seemed to be a comforting presence to this girl who had almost died in a fire two nights ago. "Thank you, Aliina," Monica whispered to the dog.

NOON SKATE

Aliina opened one eye, gazed at Monica and went back to sleep.

Monday would be the start of their lives ATF – after the fire. Monica took Suzi to school on Monday morning and arrived in the office, trying to remember what she had been working on. It seemed like she had been gone for weeks, but it had only been for the weekend. Audra came in to see how she was doing, followed by Marcia Day and then Wes. By noon, she had told the story of the fire at least five times. Wes reminded Monica that Linda Baird's deposition was being taken tomorrow in the diminished value car case by the other driver's attorney, hired by the driver's insurance company.

"Can you sit in?" Wes asked. "I think Linda will be more comfortable if she sees two of us. I'm taking their expert's dep in the afternoon." Monica thought that sounded interesting. She would listen and take notes, and if anything popped into her head that Wes might want to ask the expert, she would write it down and slip him a note. Linda's expert would be deposed on Thursday at the other attorney's office, with Wes defending it, and he invited Monica to sit in on this deposition as well.

Monica left the office for noon skate. She pulled her old, broken-down skates from the trunk and went inside, hoping they would hold her up. When she put them on, they felt like slippers compared to the stiff new boots that she had just broken in, but she knew the old boots would not support her ankles very well. She stroked around the rink, trying to feel where her balance was on the old blades, which had been sharpened so many times they were much flatter from toe to heel than the new blades. That made balance easier, but turning on one foot harder. She practiced three-turns on each foot on the circle in the center of the rink.

Janet and Julian skated up to Monica and when she stopped, they gave her a hug. "I'm so glad you and Suzi are OK," Janet said.

Callie joined them. "I am so happy to see you. We were all so worried."

They filled Monica in on who had passed or failed their dance tests on Saturday, and said that Harvey looked exhausted at the end of the day after partnering so many girls and women through their dances.

Harvey came along, gave Monica a hug and went off to teach a lesson. Brad arrived and took Monica's hand to warm up. "How do they feel?" he asked, looking at her old skates.

"I'm getting used to them," Monica said. "They sure feel different." She and Brad warmed up on the Fourteenstep and the bronze dances which Harvey put on for his student. By the end of noon skate, Monica was skating all of Brad's pre-gold dances with him. She even tried an Argentine Tango twizzle and did not trip.

She got off the ice a few minutes early to talk to Barry in the skate shop. "Didn't you just order new skates?" he said, when she told him that she needed to get another pair.

"They went up in the Southside Apartments fire," Monica said. "Will the 'new' new skates take as long, since the company has all of the measurements?"

NOON SKATE

"I'll see what I can do," Barry said. "I will put in the order right away and let's hope they come in soon. I am so sorry about what happened. I saw it on the news – just awful. And they are saying that some guy set the fire on purpose to try to kill his ex-girlfriend?"

"She is still alive," Monica said. "My neighbor Rose saw her in the park. I just can't believe that anyone would try to take out the whole building just to get back at one person. It's sickening."

"I hope he gets sent to prison for a long time," Barry said.

Monica took her old skates, put them back in the trunk of her car and returned to the office. She knew she would not get anything done if she left her door open, because everyone wanted to see and hear for themselves that she was all right. She closed the door and buried herself in work.

When she was leaving the parking lot to go home that evening, she almost turned in the direction of Southside Apartments but caught herself and turned in the opposite direction – north, towards Brad's home on the north side of town. Wiping away tears for her old home and everyone who had lost so much in the fire, she drove north. Suzi had texted her that she had a ride home from school with Gail, a classmate who lived near Brad. In fact, Gail offered to pick Suzi up in the morning and drive her home every day for the remaining two weeks of school. The seniors had one more week of regular classes, then final exams and graduation.

Suzi had been issued four graduation tickets, two of which she gave to Monica and Brad. When he looked surprised, she said, "I really want you to come. I don't know what we would be doing without you. And I could use another person in my cheering section when I walk."

Brad said he would be honored to attend Suzi's graduation, which would be held on a Wednesday evening at Center City Civic Auditorium. Suzi wanted the other two tickets to go to her grandparents, and Monica said she would call them to let them know the date, and also to let them know that she and Suzi had survived a fire. She had not heard from her parents and wondered if they knew anything about the fire. Monica had no idea if it had been on the news in the Detroit area.

"How are you doing on books and notes?" Monica asked.

"I borrowed all the books I need, and Gail is letting me borrow her notes on everything. We have all the same classes. She is a lifesaver!"

That evening on the TV news, the identity of the person who died in the fire was revealed. Monica was saddened to learn that it was Horace, as she had feared. He lived in a third-floor apartment and had apparently been overlooked by the firefighters, or maybe they could not get to him with so many other residents to rescue. She hoped he had slept through the whole thing and died peacefully. She felt badly for Maurice and his family and hoped she would be able to attend whatever memorial they planned for Horace.

In the morning, Gail arrived on time in her MINI Cooper to take Suzi to school with her. Monica hoped that Gail was a good driver – in such a small car, they would not have much of a chance if they were hit by a bus or a truck, or even another car. She waved goodbye and turned to deciding what to wear for Linda Baird's deposition, which was not hard because her choices were quite limited. She selected the black skirt, jacket, and a Kelly green blouse. She put her black slacks in a bag to change into at the rink, if she had time to get there for noon skate.

"You look nice," Brad said as she went out the door. "See you at noon."

"I hope so," Monica said. "If the deposition takes a while, I might not make it."

When she got to the office, she found a white envelope on her desk with her name on it. She opened the envelope and was surprised to find a "Thinking of You" card signed by her co-workers with personal notes from each of them, and a check. Monica's eyes almost popped out of her head when she read the amount of the check: five hundred dollars. That would cover her renters' insurance deductible. She sat down and shot everyone an email thanking them for their generous gift, wondering who had taken the time to organize this effort.

Just then Wes buzzed her and asked her to come to his office where he was preparing Linda for her deposition. Monica had never met her. Wes introduced Linda, who was nicely dressed in a dark blue pantsuit. Her short brown hair was nicely styled and she wore a black cat pin on her lapel.

"You must be a cat person," Monica said, and Linda smiled.

Wes went over with Linda what would happen in the

deposition: the court reporter would put her under oath, and then the other driver's insurance company's attorney would ask her questions. He told her not to volunteer information, and to answer the questions honestly, to the best of her recollection. If she realized later that she needed to correct an earlier answer, she would be allowed to do so. Anna buzzed Wes and told him that the court reporter and the insurance company's attorney, Cora Barron, had arrived and were in the conference room. Wes asked Linda if she was ready and she nodded.

Wes, Monica and Linda took their seats on one side of the conference table, with Linda next to the court reporter, who was seated at the end of the table. Ms. Barron sat on the other side, across from Linda. She was quite a bit older than Wes, who was still in his first year of practice after passing the Michigan Bar exam. She asked the court reporter, a middle-aged woman, to swear the witness.

Linda raised her right hand and swore to testify truthfully. Ms. Barron went over instructions similar to what Wes had already given her and reminded Linda that she needed to wait for the end of the question before she gave her answer, so they would not be talking over each other and the court reporter could take down all the words she said. She also told Linda to answer verbally and not to just nod or shake her head.

"Do you understand the instructions?" Ms. Barron asked. Linda nodded.

"You have to say yes or no," Ms. Barron reminded her, smiling.

"Oops. Yes."

"Then let's begin. Are you currently employed?"

Linda answered a few background questions and then they got into what happened on the day of the accident. Ms. Barron seemed to be trying to get Linda to say the accident was her fault, but Linda stuck to her story of what happened.

"The gray car turned right in front of me, and there was nothing I could do," she said. "There were two witnesses, and the police gave the other driver a ticket for failing to yield when she turned left in front of me. And I wasn't speeding."

"Thank you for that summary," Ms. Barron said, not sounding appreciative. "Let's turn to the repairs." She asked the court reporter to mark as an exhibit a copy of the repairs and their cost from the auto body shop that had rebuilt the entire front of Linda's car. She showed it to Linda and asked her to identify it.

"It's the repair bill that your insurance company paid for. But the problem is that now the car is worth much less because of the damage to the frame, which will appear whenever someone requests a Carfax report, and the result is that no one will pay the full Kelley Blue Book value of my brand-new car. According to my expert's report, it is now worth thousands less."

Linda had done her homework and knew what she wanted. Ms. Barron would deal with the expert who had written the report and did not ask Linda anything else. Wes thought she was probably sizing Linda up as a witness. The deposition lasted less than an hour. Ms. Barron arranged for a copy of the transcript to be sent to Wes, so he could review it for errors and Linda could make corrections and sign it. Monica took Linda to Wes' office while he escorted the court reporter and Ms. Barron to the elevator.

"You did great!" Monica told Linda. "We will let you know when the transcript is here."

Wes came in and also congratulated Linda on a job well done. "That was a dress rehearsal for trial," he said. "It was nice of them to give you one. Of course, we can still hope they come to their senses and settle this thing."

Monica left for the rink in plenty of time to get in an hour of skating. "I'm so glad you made it," Brad said. Monica was still adjusting to her old skates and took a few extra minutes to warm up, but then she skated Brad's dances with him. Later, she even got through the Viennese Waltz and Argentine Tango with no problem except that her ankles were beginning to hurt like they had before she switched to her new skates. After the session, Janet sat down with her as she was taking off her old skates. She handed Monica an envelope.

"It's not much," Janet said, "but we hope it will help you get back on your feet."

Monica opened the envelope and found a J.C. Penney's gift card for $100 from "your noon skating friends."

"Wow! Thank you!" Monica said, overwhelmed, and gave Janet a warm hug.

"We have no idea what it must be like to have to start over. But I'm sure you will have a lot of shopping to do," Janet said.

NOON SKATE

Monica thought this must be her lucky day – a check from the office and now the gift card. This would certainly help. She wondered how the other fire survivors were doing and hoped they were as fortunate.

In the afternoon, back at the office, the diminished value expert that Ms. Barron had identified on her witness list appeared at Carter Day for his scheduled deposition to be taken by Wes with a different court reporter – one from a company that he usually used. The expert's name was Perry Eastman.

Monica took a seat in the conference room next to Wes, who sat around the corner from the court reporter, who was at the end of the table. Mr. Eastman sat across from Wes, with Ms. Barron next to him.

Mr. Eastman turned out to be an employee of the insurance company and had worked as an adjuster for ten years. He had never been involved in a diminished value case but insisted, even after reviewing the report of Linda's expert, that the car had lost no value. Wes locked him in to his story and knew that his testimony would be biased, as he worked for the insurance company that did not want to pay up. In addition, Mr. Eastman would not be very persuasive because of his lack of experience in diminished value cases. Now all he had to do was hope Linda's expert could testify clearly and persuasively in her deposition on Thursday.

On her way to Brad's after work, Monica heard on the news that several of the fire survivors were living in a shelter for the homeless, with no family in the area. They had no insurance and would not be getting reimbursed for even a dime of what they had lost. She decided to donate her gift card and a share of the check from Carter Day to these families who appeared to need it far more than she did.

Horace's obituary appeared in the Center City Chronicle. Monica learned that besides Maurice and his wife and child, Horace had left a daughter, Tamara, and her three children who lived in Detroit. Horace had recently retired from a career with the U.S. Postal Service and had donated his time over the last twenty years to the Big Brothers organization and several charities in the community. His memorial service was planned for Saturday at the First Baptist Church, where Horace had been a member for thirty years.

On Thursday morning, Wes defended the deposition of Linda Baird's expert, Geraldine Long, on diminished value, taken by Cora Barron at her law firm a few blocks away in downtown Center City. Ms. Long and her husband had their own company which did nothing but prepare diminished value reports for people like Linda. They were former insurance adjusters who did not like seeing drivers getting ripped off by insurance companies and set out to do something about it. Ms. Long's report, which Wes had already provided to Ms. Barron, was detailed and well written.

After asking several questions about Ms. Long's education and professional background and qualifications, Ms. Barron showed Ms. Long a copy of her own report. Ms. Long identified it. Wes was expecting Ms. Barron to go through it line by line and try to find something wrong, but instead, Ms. Barron asked Ms. Long if she had any changes or corrections to the report. Ms. Long said no, and that was the end of the deposition. Ms. Long was a good witness and would hold up well in court. Wes hoped that Ms. Barron would realize this, and he told Monica again that the case should settle, but that the ball was in Ms. Barron's court. If the case didn't settle, Linda's trial date was set for October.

At noon skate, Monica got through her Thursday lesson with Harvey, although he commented on her old skates. "They will be OK, but I sure hope your new ones come in. Your solos seem a bit labored." At least her dances with Brad were going well and were not adversely affected by the skate change. Brad had even started working on his fourth pre-gold dance, the Starlight Waltz.

Monica checked with Barry in the skate shop before she went back to the office. He had not heard anything about her new skates but told her to be patient. "Give them a couple of weeks," he said. Monica checked the bulletin board and saw that the next test session was in July, in four weeks. She would keep her fingers crossed about the new skates getting there in time to be broken in for the test session.

When Monica got back to the office, Audra was reviewing a proposed settlement agreement between her client, Bob Ritter, and Sarah Ahmed, who had filed the charge of citizenship status discrimination against his furniture company, Ritter House. She gave Monica a copy, saying, "Ms. Ahmed was out of work for three weeks before she found a job at another furniture store that paid more than Ritter House. Her three weeks of back pay comes to $1,500, and the Office of Special Counsel wants Mr. Ritter to pay a

$1,000 civil penalty. He has agreed to the terms. Would you write up a cover letter asking him to review the agreement and sign it and return it to us. Enclose an envelope for his convenience."

Monica was glad this case was being resolved and that Mr. Ritter had decided to do the right thing. She had never met Ms. Ahmed but was sure she would be happy to get the back pay, even though she had apparently landed a better paying job after her discriminatory treatment by Ritter House.

Before going to Brad's that night, Monica swung by the local Post Office branch near Southside Apartments to see what had become of her mail – usually just junk, but once in a while there was something important. She filled out a change of address card listing Brad's address and asked if they were holding mail for Southside residents. A woman behind the counter said that they were indeed holding mail for Southside fire survivors until they provided a change of address form. "It's the least we can do," she said. "I am so sorry about what happened to you all." She went in the back and returned with a handful of mail for Monica.

Monica thanked the woman and took the mail out to her car to see what she had besides the usual junk mail. The only piece worth opening was from her mother. Inside was a check for $100. A note said, "I hope you get this and that you and Suzi are safe. Please call me."

Monica immediately dialed her mother's number. "Hi mom, we're fine," she said. "Sorry I didn't call. It's been crazy here. Thanks for the check. We are safe and staying with my skating friend and partner, Brad Peltonen." She could hear her mother breathe a sigh of relief. Monica went on, "Oh yes, and Suzi wants you and dad to come to her graduation in two weeks. I'll mail you the tickets and Brad's address, so maybe you can come to his house and we can all go together."

"We would love that," her mother said. "See you soon, then."

Monica received a text from Rose asking her if she was going to Horace's memorial service on Saturday. They agreed to meet in front of the church and enter together. Suzi had to work, and Brad offered to take her to the pool and then come to the service, but Monica said she and Rose would be fine.

Brad dropped Suzi at the pool. She thanked him and waved goodbye to him and Aliina, who was in the car waiting to go to the park with Brad. He tried to take her as often as possible to the one park in Center City that allowed dogs to run off-leash, so she could cut loose and run like a husky.

When Monica arrived at the First Baptist Church, there were no parking places left in the lot, so she ended up parking two blocks away. She texted Rose and said she was coming. Rose was having the same problem -- trying to find parking. They eventually found each other and went inside. People were crowded together in the pews, standing along both sides and in the back of the sanctuary. Monica and Rose squeezed in with people they recognized from Southside and looked around for other familiar faces. They saw dozens of people they had seen in the halls and parking lots of their old home.

Horace's son Maurice, his wife Bonita and their son Anthony were escorted in along with other relatives Monica did not know. She assumed that the woman with three young children was Horace's daughter Tamara from Detroit. The family was led to their seats in front of the congregation and the service began with a prayer, one of Horace's favorite gospel songs, and a long eulogy by the minister. He emphasized that everyone was here today to celebrate Horace's life, and talked about all the time Horace had devoted to church and to volunteer work, and how they would all remember him for his smile and his willingness to help anyone in need. Monica could certainly vouch for that. She would miss him and could see that his passing was leaving a huge hole in the hearts of the many other people he had touched. She and Rose were both blinking back tears.

There were more hymns and prayers, and then the attendees were invited to share a meal with the family in the church hall. Monica and Rose went through a receiving line where Maurice and the other relatives were standing. Maurice thanked her for coming, and she again told him how sorry she was and how kind Horace had been to her.

"That's our dad," said Maurice's sister, Tamara. "I'm glad you knew him."

Monica and Rose found seats at a table with other Southside residents who were talking about the many ways Horace had helped them over the years – helping with their cars that wouldn't start, shoveling them out of their parking spaces after a big snow storm, providing extra food to families in need; the list went on and on. The Southside survivors also compared notes on how they were all doing after the fire and expressed great gratitude for their survival. There was plenty of food in the church hall, so the Southside table got in line and returned to share platters of chicken, sweet potatoes, salad and bread. They exchanged phone numbers and promised to stay in touch and to help each other if anyone needed anything. Monica thought that it was too bad that it took a funeral to bring all these people together, but she was glad they were re-united. She and Rose left the church together, hugged one more time, and walked away, blinking back more tears.

Chapter Five

Over the next week, Monica and Suzi settled into a routine with Brad. He got up first, took Aliina out for her morning business, fed her and then set out some breakfast things: hard-boiled eggs, toast, cereal, orange juice, milk and coffee. Suzi would grab a few bites and head out the door when Gail swung by to pick her up. It was exam week, so the girls studied together every night at Gail's house.

Monica and Brad had breakfast together and she kissed him goodbye, drove to work, and met up with him later at noon skate. They worked hard on his pre-gold dances and she on her gold dances. Monica's ankles ached from the old boots' lack of support, and she checked every day with Barry to see if her new skates had come in, but there was no sign of them. The best part of the week was receiving a check for $5,000 from her renters' insurance company, for the furniture and clothing and other personal items she and Suzi had lost in the fire. She deposited the check, relieved that she could now afford to buy more clothes and a laptop for Suzi, which she would need for college. And she arranged for the full amount of her $500 check from Carter Day and the $100 gift card from the noon skaters to go to the Southside Survivors Fund, which had been set up to help those most in need of assistance. She remembered when Suzi was a baby, after they had left Hannah's House, when she had at times been without a job, insurance or a place to stay. During those times, she had relied on the generosity of strangers, and now she was in a position to give back.

Suzi finished her last exam and was issued a cap and gown to wear at graduation. The graduates were expected to show up at the Center City Civic Auditorium the day before the ceremony, for a run-through and instructions about where to line up and where to sit.

On the big night, Gail picked Suzi up with her cap and gown and they drove to the Auditorium to find their places. Monica's parents arrived at Brad's house just after Suzi had left and met Brad for the first time. Aliina sniffed the new visitors, decided they were harmless, and went off to chew on one of her toys.

"You have a beautiful home," Mrs. Jones told Brad. "The trees and flowers out back are lovely. It must be nice in the winter, too."

Mr. Jones remarked that it looked like a nice neighborhood and thanked Brad for taking in Monica and Suzi.

"It's my pleasure," Brad said. "I have been enjoying their company, and so has Aliina." The dog's ears perked up, and then she went back to her favorite toy.

Brad and Mr. Jones talked about dogs for a few minutes, until Monica said, "We better get going if we want to get good seats."

Brad drove them all to the auditorium and they found seats in the upper level reserved for guests. The graduates would all sit on the main floor. Soon, all of the upper level seats were full and the friends and families of the graduates waited eagerly for the students to process in. Monica spotted Suzi and waved. After some musical selections by the Center City High School Choir, and remarks from the principal and others, the graduates began their walks across the stage, where the principal handed them fake diplomas that would later be replaced by the real thing. When Suzi's turn came and her name was announced, Brad, Monica and her parents jumped up and cheered. Suzi walked; Monica cried.

Her baby had made it – through difficult years when Monica wasn't sure where the next meal would be coming from, through a near drowning when Suzi was a child, through the recent fire, and now through high school. She was so proud of her daughter for all of her accomplishments, in swimming, school and life. She was a good kid who had never been in trouble and had compassion for others. What more could a mother want?

Brad sensed her emotions and put his arm around Monica. "Congratulations to you, too," he said. "You should be proud of both of you for this day."

They took Suzi out for dinner after the ceremony and her grandparents presented her with a check as a graduation gift. "Let us hear from you, dear," they said, before leaving Brad's house. Suzi and Gail went to a graduation party at a friend's house, and Monica and Brad had a glass of wine on the deck.

"She will be off to college soon," Monica said. "I don't know where the time went."

*****

The following week, Suzi started her summer job at the 50-meter outdoor pool in Center City. She arranged for transportation with another lifeguard who lived near Brad. They were scheduled to work from 8 a.m. to 4:30 p.m. Monday through Friday.

Noon skate was still running in the summer, but the rink had children's ice-skating camps in the building, making for a more chaotic atmosphere. Groups of children would take to the ice for lessons and general skating, except for their lunch hour and a movie, when noon skate and a one-hour adult general session would be held. Harvey had insisted on this time because his adult students needed to continue their progress during the summer. The Center City Skating Club ran four sessions every evening, Monday through Thursday, an hour each for low-level freestyle, high-level freestyle, low dance and high dance. Brad paid for both himself and Monica to skate high dance all four nights to get in some extra ice time.

The evening high dance sessions were very crowded, with young skaters and adults all working on silvers through golds. Coaches could play whatever music was needed for lessons, as on noon skate, and those doing the dance being played had the right of way. Harvey had to devote most of this time to his younger students yet continued teaching Monica and Brad on Thursdays at noon skate.

After a week of the summer schedule, just before the Fourth of July, Monica's ankles were hurting worse than ever from the old skates' lack of support, and her knees ached from all the extra sessions. She was starting to wonder if she was too old for this, when her new skates came in. She tried them on in the skate shop and told Barry that they were fine, but she groaned inwardly thinking about the break-in process that lay ahead of her. There was no way these skates would be ready to wear for the test session just one week away. She told Barry to go ahead and mount the new blades and she would pick the skates up on Monday, after the Fourth of July weekend.

Monica and Brad attended the Center City Independence Day celebration at Riverview Park, where a fireworks display was scheduled for 10 p.m. They left Aliina at home, where she would not be frightened by the loud noises, and enjoyed an evening of patriotic music by the Center City Community Band and the fireworks, which were the best in many years. Suzi missed the festivities because she was asked to lifeguard for a special Independence Day event at the pool, for which she would be paid double time.

On Monday, Monica tried out her new skates for a few minutes to test the placement of the blades. She gave them to Barry and told him they were fine. He would put in some extra screws and she would pick up the skates the following day. She decided to skate in her old skates for the rest of the week, until the test session Friday night, because it was too hard to go back and forth between the new and the old pair. Brad was set to test all of his pre-golds, though the Starlight Waltz was a long shot. The Starlight was going well with Monica, as were the other three dances -- the Kilian, Paso Doble and Blues -- so Harvey signed a last-minute test application for the additional dance. Monica was planning to test the Viennese Waltz and Argentine Tango, which she had planned to take the day of the fire. She purchased a new black skating dress from the skate shop, because all of her skating dresses had been destroyed in the fire. Black was traditional for testing, and would go with whatever color Harvey and Brad were wearing.

On Friday, Monica left work early to get to the rink in plenty of time to warm up with Brad, who would test first, along with other pre-gold skaters. Harvey spent most of the warmup time with his pre-gold female students but had time to remind Brad to bend his knees, listen to the music, and trust his hours of practice to get him through. Monica thought that timing had never been a problem for Brad, but during a test, when adrenaline was flowing, everyone had a tendency to rush and be slightly ahead of the music.

Brad's first dance would be the Kilian. He and Monica warmed it up with the other testers and then got off the ice until it was Brad's turn. When his name was called, he and Monica stepped onto the ice and stroked together to their starting point in front of the judges, who were seated behind the boards on the same side of the rink. Monica and Brad would be skating four patterns of the dance together, and then Brad would do two patterns by himself.

Brad squeezed Monica's hand and she gave him a reassuring smile. The music started and they struck off together, doing the introductory steps, then the outside edges that Brad was now doing very well and into progressives and the choctaw. No problem. Three more patterns. Monica thought the dance felt good. She skated off the ice to allow for Brad's solo. He was on time and on pattern, and Harvey told him, "Good job."

There were several others testing the Kilian and then the warmup music for the Paso Doble was played. Brad and Monica repeated the process, with Brad again skating well.

On the Blues test with Monica, he started to rush a bit on the introduction, so Monica told him to slow down, and he was fine. The Starlight went well, much to Monica's surprise. Harvey had taught Brad how to make the end pattern easy for the partner to do; Brad and Monica made it look effortless. Brad's solo was also very strong.

"Well, I did my best," Brad said as he got off the ice after his Starlight Waltz solo. "If I failed, there is always another test session."

The pre-gold testers sat nervously waiting for their

results while the Zamboni resurfaced the ice for the gold tests. Mrs. Anderson, the test chairperson, finally appeared and handed out copies of the test papers, one paper from each of the three judges on the panel for each dance. She passed to Brad a handful of paperwork and he glanced through it, looking for "Pass" or "Fail" at the bottom of each page. He found three passes on the Kilian and Paso Doble with extra points, three passes on the Blues with the passing minimum score, and two passes on the Starlight Waltz, all that he needed to pass that dance! Monica and Harvey were looking over Brad's shoulder.

"Nice job. Congratulations!" Harvey said, shaking his student's hand. "And you, too, Monica. You had a lot to do with this. Now you can start partnering Brad on his golds!"

Monica gave Brad a big hug and told him she was very proud of him. She knew he had put in the time on his pre-golds and couldn't wait to start working on gold dances with him. But now she had to try to pass her own gold dances. The Zamboni finished its job, the ice dried, and Monica took the ice with Harvey to warm up her Viennese Waltz. She still felt warmed up from skating Brad's pre-golds, but her ankles were starting to hurt. "Just two more dances," she told herself, determined to get through this.

Monica was the third person to test the Viennese, and also the third student to skate it with Harvey. He had time to recover while each student was skating her solo, so Monica was not worried about him wearing out. When it was her turn, Harvey told her to stay close to him, bend her knees and push. They sailed through the required two patterns of the dance together, and Harvey escorted Monica to her starting position for her solo before he skated off the ice.

Monica took a deep breath, listened to the music and struck off on the correct beat. She could feel her knees shaking when she went past the judges but this was nothing new. She kept going and did her two solo patterns, wondering if they were big enough to satisfy the judges, who were looking for more flow and deeper edges than they had seen from the pre-gold skaters earlier.

The Argentine Tango was next, and Monica was first. She and Harvey completed the required two patterns of the dance together, and she thought they had gone well – even the twizzles. Harvey could assist her twizzle when he was skating with her by giving her an impetus, but she would not have this assistance on her solo.

Harvey again escorted Monica to her starting position for her solo and got off the ice. Monica felt a bit wobbly on this dance but she got through the first pattern and twizzle. On the second pattern, her confidence evaporated moments before the twizzle and she almost tripped. She caught herself and finished the dance on time and on pattern. Harvey said, "Nice save on the twizzle."

Monica took off her skates, dried the blades and went up in the stands to sit with Brad and watch the other Argentine Tango, Quickstep and Westminster Waltz tests – the other two gold dances that she hoped to test before the end of the year. Harvey partnered most of the students through these tests, and when the last one was over, he looked like he needed a vacation.

NOON SKATE

Mrs. Anderson, the test chairperson, gave Monica her test papers which she handed to Brad, not daring to look. "Always another test session," Monica said, fearing for the worst.

"You passed the Viennese by two judges and got one pass on the Argentine," Brad said, just as Harvey came over and took a look at the papers and the judges' comments. The judge who had failed Monica's Viennese commented on her lack of flow but only failed her by a tenth of a point. The other two judges had passed her, so she had this dance out of the way. One of the same judges passed her Argentine with comments on the twizzle and the other two failed her by two tenths because of it.

"That will be easy to fix in your new skates," Harvey said. "The rest of the dance was fine. So, let's keep working on it but spend most of our time on the West and the Quick."

Monica was relieved that she had one gold dance out of the way and could start breaking in her new skates on Monday, switching off between them and her old ones like she had done before. Brad took Monica out to dinner to celebrate and to thank her for getting him through his pre-golds. He asked her if she would like to go to dinner and dancing at the Center City Club next weekend, and she said she would love to, hoping that her knees and feet would feel better by that time.

The next week was a busy one at Carter Day, with Audra, Wes and two other attorneys giving her new research assignments. One of the paralegals at the firm had retired, so Monica and Linsey Wang, the other paralegal on the fifth floor, inherited her work and had to take up the slack. Linsey, who had been there only two years, said she had never worked this hard in her ten years as a paralegal. Linsey added, "Maybe we should go to law school so we can get paid four times as much for doing the same work the attorneys are doing."

Law school had been in the back of Monica's mind for a while, but with Suzi going to college in the fall, and trying to recover financially from the fire, she didn't think it would be possible any time soon. Three years of law school would be a long haul, and right now all of her spare funds were going to skating. Any further education would have to wait. Besides, Monica thought her brain would still be good for a while but maybe her knees wouldn't, so she wanted to get her gold ice dance medal before her knees gave out.

The new skates were breaking in nicely and Monica and Brad enjoyed working together on the Viennese Waltz with Harvey. Monica worked on the Westminster Waltz and Quickstep on her own lessons with Harvey and kept putting mileage on her solos. The evening high dance sessions were difficult after work, but the extra time was paying off.

By Friday, Monica was ready for dinner and dancing with Brad. She wore a new red dress with matching shoes and earrings, courtesy of the insurance money. Brad wore a coat and red tie. The waiter showed them to the table where they had sat on their first date, in March. It seemed like ages ago. This time they knew each other so much better. They ordered and Brad asked Monica to dance while they waited for their meals. He led her easily through a foxtrot, a waltz, a tango and a swing. The house band seemed to be playing with extra zest this evening, and Brad was lighter on his feet than usual, though Monica thought she felt him shaking a few times and wondered what was wrong.

The conversation over their dinner and a glass of wine was more relaxed and they enjoyed the meal, getting up occasionally to dance. For dessert, they ordered a piece of chocolate cake to share, and Brad told Monica to divide it up. When she cut into it with a knife, she hit something hard.

"What the heck?" she thought, wondering if someone's tooth had fallen into the cake. When she examined the hard object on the plate, she found, to her surprise, a diamond ring! She stared at Brad.

"I love you," he said, getting down on one knee. "Will you marry me?" The band stopped playing and everyone in the Club turned to listen to what Monica would say.

"Yes, yes, yes!" she said, and everyone applauded. She gave Brad a big hug and he led her to the dance floor again. The band played a waltz that Brad had requested earlier, providing he got the answer from Monica he was hoping for -- "Could I have This Dance for the Rest of My Life?"

Monica had not been expecting Brad to pop the question for a while. He said, "I know this might be a bit soon, but we have been together for four months now, and I know everything I need to know to want to make you a part of my life forever." He was thrilled that she had said yes without hesitation. "We can make it as long an engagement as you want."

They went back to their table, and Monica told Brad she

wanted to be with him always, and the sooner they tied the knot, the better. She had been afraid that with Suzi and her suddenly moving in, Brad would decide he preferred the bachelor life, but the new arrangement had worked out so well.

"Well, the soonest would be at City Hall next week," Brad joked, but Monica thought that sounded like a great idea.

"Then we could have a big party on the ice for all of our noon skating friends," she said. Brad agreed that would be nice. He also wanted to take Monica to the Upper Peninsula to meet his family, maybe during the last two weeks of the summer when the rink closed down.

"I usually go up north then," he said. "I can't wait for you to meet everyone, and they will throw us a big party. We can meet them all and then go for a honeymoon on Isle Royale. Have you been there?"

Monica had never been to Michigan's wilderness national park located in the northwest corner of Lake Superior, northwest of the Keweenaw Peninsula, near Michigan's border with Canada. She thought it sounded very romantic and couldn't think of a better plan.

They arranged to go to City Hall on Friday, in one week, so they would have a chance to pick out wedding apparel and rings and take care of other last minute details, like Monica requesting the day off from work. When they got back to Brad's house, they told Suzi the news and she gave them both a big hug. "I'm so happy," she said. "I want to be there at City Hall. I hope I can find someone to sub for me."

NOON SKATE

Suzi asked Tony, one of the weekend lifeguards, to work for her on Friday and he agreed. Monica and Suzi went off to the Center City Mall to buy new dresses for the occasion. Monica selected a beautiful white tea length gown and Suzi chose a turquoise dress, and they picked out matching shoes and accessories.

Monica went to the office on Monday morning and filled out a leave slip. For the reason, she wrote, "Wedding Bells." Soon, the news was all over the office.

"I'm so happy for you," Audra said, admiring her beautiful engagement ring. Others stopped by to express the same sentiments, and Monica got very little work done on Monday or during the rest of the week. On Thursday, she got an email that seemed to be sent to everyone on the fifth floor, telling her to report to the conference room for an all-hands-on-deck meeting. She thought that was strange for a Thursday, but grabbed a legal pad and pen and headed for the conference room. When she opened the door, the room was dark and for an instant she thought she must have misread the email. Then her co-workers turned on the lights and yelled, "Surprise!"

The conference room table was piled high with gifts for Monica's surprise wedding shower. She couldn't believe they had gotten it together this fast. "Wow, I don't know what to say! Thank you – this is amazing."

"Congratulations on marrying a Finn!" said Audra, who was half Finnish.

There were refreshments for all to enjoy, and Monica opened the many gifts – things for the kitchen, bathroom and bedroom, as well as more personal items and gift cards. She called Brad to tell him what was going on and he couldn't believe it either. Monica needed help getting her gifts out to the car, and Brad helped her bring it all into the house when she got there after work. She reminded herself to write thank you notes to everyone.

In the morning, Monica and Suzi dressed in their wedding apparel, Brad put on a tux, and they all climbed into the Regal. Although they were nervous, they made it to City Hall in one piece and went to the hall where the ceremony would take place. Suzi recorded everything on her cell phone as Brad and Monica exchanged wedding vows and became husband and wife.

They had tried to keep their wedding plans a secret, and their skating friends had no idea what they were up to. After leaving City Hall, they picked up a cake Monica had ordered and took it to the rink. They asked Barry, who was speechless when he saw them in their wedding attire, to hide it for them until the end of the session, and they put on their skates. Brad stepped onto the ice first in his tuxedo and extended his hand to Monica, still wearing her wedding dress, while Suzi videotaped. They got on the ice and one by one, the noon skaters turned to watch, realized what was going on, and started applauding. Someone put on the Viennese Waltz, which Monica and Brad skated together while everyone stood at the boards and cheered them on. When they finished, they invited everyone to join them for cake after the session.

The wedding cake was a big hit, and the skaters were

thrilled that Monica and Brad were sharing it with them. Janet and Julian gave them big hugs and toasted them with bottles of water, wishing them many years of skating and life together. When they got home, Brad carried Monica over the threshold and they went inside to enjoy some afternoon delights.

Suzi took Aliina for a walk and spent the rest of the day with Gail and some other friends from school, to talk about their college plans. She was starting to wonder whether going away to college was a good idea, with all that had happened. Gail was going to Michigan State and Alexis, another friend, was going to the University of Michigan. They were both excited and had been gathering things for their dorm rooms, which Suzi had not even thought about. Maybe she should just stay home, go to Mid-Michigan University or Center City Community College and share her room with Aliina. She had grown used to the dog sleeping on her bed and had taken over some of Brad's dog walking duties. Then again, she had always wanted to go away to college and had been looking forward to swimming on the women's team at Winter College. Gail and Alexis were very positive and assured Suzi that they would be in touch with her, and they would all get together during breaks from school. She felt better after spending some time with them and decided to plan on going to freshman orientation at Winter College in August.

Brad and Monica woke up on Saturday, their first day as husband and wife. Suzi had left a note that she had taken the car to work, which she had been doing for the past several

Saturdays, to sub for other lifeguards and to make some extra money. She also said she had taken Aliina out and fed her. Monica was happy that she could spend the morning relaxing with Brad. They both called their parents and told them the exciting news.

"My folks say welcome to the family!" Brad told Monica after he finished speaking with his parents.

"Mine too," Monica said. She also texted Margie and Rose and got some congratulatory messages in return.

Brad made reservations at the Rock Harbor Lodge on Isle Royale for their honeymoon in August and they talked about their schedules for the next four weeks before their trip to the Upper Peninsula.

Monica and Brad skated every day at noon and on the evening high dance sessions, with Monica partnering Brad on his lessons with Harvey and whenever the Viennese Waltz and the Argentine Tango were played. She also continued working on her Argentine solo when Brad worked on his, and they both worked on their solo Quicksteps and Westminster Waltzes.

Skating continued to be a welcome break for Monica from the office, which was still very busy with one less paralegal. Monica wondered why they were not interviewing people for the open position. She did her best to get as much done during the regular workday as she could, so she would have time to skate at noon and be home in time for dinner with Brad and Suzi.

Monica's new skates were breaking in well, and her ankles no longer ached after skating. She could feel her edges getting deeper and her stroking more powerful. With the new blades, she was turning her twizzle with greater ease and her confidence was growing. She looked forward to the test session in August.

Harvey signed the test applications for Monica's Argentine Tango, Quickstep and Westminster Waltz, and put Brad up for the Viennese Waltz. His other dances were coming along well, but he needed more mileage on them. Brad understood and hoped he would at least get the one gold dance out of the way. Monica hoped she would pass one more dance – if she passed all three, she would be a gold dance medalist, but that was too much to hope for right now -- she had already been so fortunate!

*****

Monica and Suzi drove up to Winter College in Winter Grove for Suzi's freshman orientation on the third Saturday in August. They sat in a large gymnasium and heard welcoming speeches from the dean and other college officials. Then the students were divided into small groups for tours of the campus, placement testing, individual meetings with a counselor, financial aid sessions and registration for classes. The parents were taken on their own tours of the campus and heard talks from campus security personnel and academic counselors. In between sessions, there was a lunch break where the students could sample the dorm food and mingle with other incoming freshmen. Parents were invited to eat lunch on campus to sample what their children would be eating for a year. At the end of the day, Suzi had collected a bag full of material which she read over in the car on the way home.

"So, what classes did you sign up for?" Monica asked.

"Freshman composition, psychology, college algebra, how to be a student, and a women's studies class that sounded interesting." Suzi seemed happy with her classes and Monica was relieved that Winter College seemed to be a good fit for her daughter.

*****

The August ice dance test session was set for the following Saturday, the last day Center City Ice Arena would be open for the summer. The tests would start in the morning with preliminary dances and work their way up to gold. Janet and Julian had just gotten their gold dance judging appointments and would be judging silver through gold dances. Other judges would cover the lower level dances. Harvey again would be very busy, partnering over fifty dance tests during the day. For his efforts, he would earn a partner fee from each skater, which they paid to him in addition to their test fees submitted to the Center City Skating Club.

Test day finally came. Monica again wore her black dress, and Brad wore black pants and a royal blue shirt. They drove to the rink together in Brad's car. When they arrived, they checked in with the monitor who said the test session was on schedule. Monica and Brad put on their skates and did some stretching. The pre-gold tests had just finished, and the Zamboni was coming out to resurface the ice for the gold tests. The Viennese Waltz tests would go first.

NOON SKATE

When the Viennese warmup music started, Monica and Brad were ready. They smiled at each other and skated the required three patterns of the dance, which went well. Brad was on time and skated deep edges with plenty of flow. As he was skating his solo, Monica thought she saw Janet and Julian smiling with approval.

The Argentine Tango tests were next. Harvey warmed up one pattern with each of his three skaters who were testing the dance. This time Monica was last. The first two testers were teenage girls who were very strong skaters. Monica hoped that would not put her in a bad position, with the judges comparing her to them. When it was her turn, she skated to her starting spot with Harvey. He squeezed her hand and they struck off on the introductory steps. Monica felt much stronger this time. Her solo also felt good. Both twizzles went well, and when she got off the ice, Harvey said, "Good job."

The warmup for the Quickstep was next. Monica had been afraid of the choctaw in this dance until Harvey told her to put her back against his arm after the turn. This resulted in her weight being in the right place and she was able to stay with Harvey on the next couple of steps without pulling apart from him. They stayed together beautifully on the test and Monica took the ice to do her solo. The first solo choctaw was fine, but she started to lose concentration on the second one, had her weight too far forward, and scraped noisily with her toe pick as she was going past the judges -- not the sound or sight she wanted to leave them with.

On the Westminster Waltz test, she skated well with

Harvey and thought the solo had gone well, but she would have to wait and see what the judges thought. She took off her skates and Brad joined her to wait for their results. With all the testers, this took forever. Finally, Mrs. Anderson appeared and passed out the papers. Brad looked at his and said, "Passed it! Thanks to you, Monica." All three judges had given Brad the minimum passing score on the Viennese – his first gold dance.

Monica sorted through her papers and was thrilled to find that she had passed the Argentine by all three judges. Janet had written, "Nice twizzle" and drawn a smiling face on her judging sheet. One judge had passed Monica's Quickstep and all three had failed her Westminster Waltz. The problem on the Quickstep solo was the choctaw and on the West, the judges wanted to see more flow and deeper edges.

Harvey congratulated all of his students who had passed anything, told them to have a good two weeks off and he would see them in September. He was headed for two weeks of relaxation at a resort in Virginia Beach and in North Carolina, where he had family.

Monica couldn't wait to rest her aching knees and have two weeks alone with Brad. They had planned to take Aliina to the U.P. but Suzi begged them to leave the dog home with her. She didn't want to be in the house alone for her last two weeks of work and promised to walk Aliina and feed her every day. Brad knew his husky would be in good hands, and he and Monica planned to leave on Monday morning.

Chapter Six

"What am I going to put my things in?" Monica asked Brad. "My suitcases were destroyed in the fire and I haven't had a chance to get any new luggage."

"Not a problem," Brad said. "I have plenty of suitcases. What color do you prefer?" He led Monica to the attic where his luggage collection was piled high. She selected a medium size blue suitcase, and Brad hauled down a large black bag and a strange looking black case.

"What is that?" Monica asked as Brad opened it to reveal an accordion. "Wow!" she exclaimed. "Do you play?"

Brad took the instrument out and played a familiar tune.

Monica thought maybe that was why he had such good timing on the ice – he had musical training!

"I took lessons when I was a kid," he said. My dad and I used to play at dances sometimes in the U.P. He taught me all the old-time Finnish tunes that he learned from his father. My cousin Don used to play the mandolin and my sisters Kaarina and Gena played violins. I'm hoping I can make some music up there with some of them."

Monica couldn't wait to hear the Peltonen family musicians. She was still learning new things about Brad and was looking forward to seeing where he had come from and meeting her new in-laws.

They finished packing and loaded up Brad's Buick Regal. Suzi was preparing to take Aliina for her morning walk before she went to work at the pool, and she wished her mother and Brad a safe trip. Monica and Suzi promised each other they would at least send a text every day.

Brad and Monica agreed that Monica would drive the first leg of the trip, until they got across the Mackinac Bridge, and then Brad would take over for the rest of the drive to his parents' home in Hillside, about three hours farther along two-lane back roads in the U.P. Soon, Monica was driving up I-75 in very light traffic. Brad snoozed in the passenger seat. They stopped for gas in Mackinaw City, the last town on the Lower Peninsula side of the Straits of Mackinac, a five-mile stretch of water connecting Lake Huron to the east and Lake Michigan to the west. Since there was a coffee shop near the gas station, they parked the car and had a light lunch. Brad offered to drive from there so they wouldn't have to stop again. He was refreshed after his nap and said he loved driving across the bridge.

The Mackinac Bridge, completed in 1957, is a five-mile-long suspension bridge spanning the Straits. Monica had been across it a few times as a child but had forgotten how breathtaking it was. Trusting Brad's driving completely, she enjoyed watching the ore boats on the water far below and trying to find the historic Grand Hotel through the trees on Mackinac Island to the east. The bridge had four narrow lanes which were all busy at this time of year, with vacationers going up north or returning to their homes in the Lower Peninsula.

Brad paid the toll on the U.P side and drove off along a two-lane road that ran along the shore of Lake Michigan and its sandy beaches, where families with children were stopping to get their feet wet. Brad seemed to be in a hurry to see his folks but drove carefully, passing other cars only when it was clear and never on a double yellow line. After a couple of hours, Brad turned north and took a series of back roads until he finally drove up to an old farmhouse.

"We made it!" he said. "I hope someone is home. I did tell them we would be coming, but we made such good time, they may not be ready for us." It was 4 p.m.

Monica noticed several cars parked out back but didn't say anything. She followed Brad to the door where he rapped a few times and then let himself in. "Hello!" he called. There was no answer, so he led Monica through the large living room and opened a door into the dining room.

"Surprise!" yelled at least fifteen people, jumping out

from every direction. Monica jumped a foot in the air and then started laughing. Brad hugged the closest woman and said, "Mom! We made it. This is my wife, Monica."

Brad's mother, Myra Peltonen, was a trim woman in her late sixties with blonde hair and green eyes. Her hair was pulled up into a neat bun and she sported gold wire rimmed glasses. She gave Monica a hug and introduced her to Brad's father, Arthur Peltonen, also in his late sixties with grey hair and a mustache, in jeans and a plaid shirt. Brad's younger sisters, Kaarina and Gena, and their husbands and children were introduced, and finally, Patsy, the widow of Brad's cousin Don who had died earlier in the year. Patsy introduced her children, twelve-year-old Donnie and fourteen-year-old Molly.

Monica was certainly surprised to be meeting so many new people all at once. She hoped she would remember all of their names. Myra offered everyone coffee, tea, milk or water, and a selection of cookies. "But don't spoil your appetites. The girls and I are making pasties in the kitchen. Monica, would you like to help?"

Monica followed Myra, Gena, Kaarina and Patsy to the large kitchen where they had been rolling out the dough to form into circles. Meat, potatoes, carrots, onions and rutabaga were being cut into pieces. Monica grabbed a knife and joined in. She had never made pasties and wanted to pay close attention so she could make these meat pies at home. Myra explained that pasties had been introduced by miners from Cornwall, England, and that Finnish miners in the U.P. used to carry them, steaming hot, in their lunch pails.

NOON SKATE

The meat, potatoes, carrots, onions, rutabaga and seasonings were mixed together and spooned into the circles of dough, which were then folded over. Two of the children -- Gena's daughters Iris and Violet – appeared, grabbed forks and started pressing the dough together around the edges, like a piecrust. They had obviously done this before and had mastered the task.

"Thank you, girls," Myra said. "Now you can stab the pasties so they won't explode in the oven." The girls used their forks to pierce the top of each pasty. Myra then placed the pasties on baking sheets and popped them into the oven. She set a timer for one hour, and the women went into the empty dining room.

"Where did they all go?" Monica asked.

"To the sauna," Gena replied. "It's out back. The men and boys will get it all ready, go to sauna together and then it will be our turn – if you like."

The women sat down for coffee until the men returned and told the women that the sauna was all theirs. Monica followed the women and girls to a small building in back of the house. Inside the door there was a pile of towels. Each woman removed her clothes, grabbed a towel, showered, and went into the sauna, the Finnish steam bath enjoyed by so many worldwide. Brad's father and uncle had built saunas for each of their homes. Gena and Kaarina said they looked forward to visiting their mom and dad because they didn't have saunas in their own homes, and their parents' sauna was the best one in the U.P.

The temperature in the sauna was 180 degrees

Fahrenheit, so it didn't take long for the women to start sweating. Monica wondered how long she could stay in there and was almost ready to take a break, when Myra said, "That will do it for me. You can stay as long as you want, Monica."

But Monica followed Myra into the showers and changing room. They took a quick shower, got dressed and went back to the house. The other women soon followed. The aroma of baking pasties filled the house, and Monica realized that she was very hungry. She helped set the table and pour milk for the children.

The pasties were delicious. Bottles of ketchup were passed around and applied generously to the pasties, and the hungry family devoured them. Monica had never tasted anything so good.

For dessert, Myra had made an apple cobbler, served with vanilla ice cream. Monica took a small piece and savored every bite. Coffee was served with dessert, and the conversation was all about what was going on in the lives of Brad, his sisters and his cousin's widow, Patsy. They talked about people Monica did not know - old teachers, neighbors, and classmates, and she made a mental note to ask Brad later who these people were.

After dinner, everyone went into the living room, which they called the front room, and musical instruments were pulled out from every corner. Brad ran to the car to get his accordion. Patsy, Monica, the children, and the husbands of Kaarina and Gena watched while Brad and his father pulled up chairs next to each other with their accordions. Kaarina and Gena stood behind them with their violins. Myra stood next to Arthur and nodded for them all to start. She sang in Finnish while they accompanied her on some of their favorite Finnish songs – *Satumaa, Emma, Kulkurin Valssi, Villiruusu* and many more. Monica enjoyed the impromptu concert. Patsy looked like she was going to cry, hearing all the songs her husband Don used to play, and Monica reached out to touch her shoulder. Patsy said she was fine, but Monica, a new bride, didn't know how she could be, having lost her husband so recently.

The children had been doing their own dancing to the music, some of which Monica knew were waltzes and polkas. Brad had mentioned the *jenkka*, or schottische, which she hoped he would teach her to dance one day, but for now she just listened. She sat back and enjoyed the music and the family camaraderie.

After an hour of music, Gena and Kaarina started packing up their violins and saying their goodbyes. They and their families climbed into their cars to drive back to their homes in the Marquette area, a half hour away. "We'll see you in a few days," Gena said. "Welcome to the family, Monica, and congratulations for getting our brother to settle down." Monica hugged Kaarina and Gena and waved goodbye for the evening.

Patsy and her two children got in their car to drive back to their home a few miles away. She invited Brad and Monica to stop by and see the dogs tomorrow. Monica remembered that Aliina had come from Don and Patsy's farm.

Brad brought in the suitcases he and Monica had packed, which were still in the trunk of his car. They sat and talked to his parents for a while and showed them the video Suzi had taken of the wedding and the party at the ice rink afterwards. Finally, Brad and Monica said good night and took their suitcases upstairs.

"This used to be my room," Brad said, putting the suitcases down. "Gena and Kaarina shared a room next door, and my parents' room is across the hall. Make yourself at home."

As they were unpacking, Monica said, "I really enjoyed the music. You are so lucky to have a family that can enjoy making music together."

They got ready for bed, pulled back a quilt and crawled into the double bed. "Something's wrong," muttered Brad, and Monica was thinking the same thing. Their feet were hitting the quilt instead of the sheet. They threw back the quilt to find that someone had short-sheeted the bed – a prank on the newlyweds, so the sheets only covered their upper bodies and not their legs and feet. Brad suspected Gena and Kaarina, but then he heard his dad's voice out in the hall, "How ya doing in there? Need any sheets?" He was roaring with laughter.

"Thanks, dad," Brad called out. "We're fine." He and Monica got out of bed, pulled off the short-sheeted sheets and remade the bed the right way. "I'm so sorry," he said to Monica, hoping she was not going to hate his family. She gave him a big hug, happy to be part of all this, pranks and all.

NOON SKATE

In the morning, Monica and Brad enjoyed a delicious breakfast of scrambled eggs, hot cereal, and toast with homemade strawberry jam, fresh blueberries, orange juice and coffee. After breakfast, Brad's parents gave them a set of Finnish *Iittala* dinnerware as a wedding present. As they examined the beautiful patterns on the matching cups, bowls and plates, Myra explained that the collection was called *Tanssi* which means "dance" in Finnish.

"It's beautiful," Monica said, admiring the pieces. "And perfect for us. We will think of you every time we use it."

Brad said he would pick up the gift on their way back from Isle Royale, so it wouldn't get stolen or broken, and he also left his accordion there. He and Monica loaded their suitcases into the car and headed for Don's farm, for a visit with Patsy.

When they drove up to Patsy's house, they were welcomed by at least a dozen huskies that looked just like Aliina. Patsy came out to try to herd the dogs back into a barn, but Monica said they were fine and let them sniff her, wondering if they smelled Aliina, their sister or cousin, on her clothing.

"They're beautiful," Monica said. "I would love to see them run in the snow sometime."

Motioning to the barn, Patsy said, "I'll show you the sled, and the puppies! Come with me."

Monica and Brad followed Patsy into the barn where there was a large sled and a smaller one that the dogs could pull in the snow. "The kids love to go dogsledding," she said. "There are trails in the woods and on Hillside Lake when it freezes over in the winter. They could pull you, too. And Aliina could help!"

Patsy led them to a stall in the back of the barn where a husky was nursing four puppies in a large dog bed on the floor. "This is Vera, Aliina's mom," Patsy said. "She had these puppies about a month ago – two females and two males. We haven't named them yet."

Monica wanted to pick up every puppy and give it some love, but she could see they were busy getting nourishment from their mother. "They are so sweet," Monica said. "What will you do with them?"

Patsy said they might keep one or two and sell the others to one of the many sled dog teams in the U.P. "Our dogs are in big demand," she said. "We have people on a waiting list to get them."

Patsy also showed them Aliina's father, Veikko, who was playing with the other dogs. "You can see where Aliina gets her energy," Patsy said.

"I'd like to come back at Christmas," Brad said. "We could take the dogs out and see if Aliina remembers what to do." Monica knew he made a trip up north to see his family every winter and she nodded in agreement. She would like to see Aliina working with the other dogs, doing what they loved to do in the snow, and she knew Suzi would too. They went in the house for coffee and talked to Patsy for a while. She gave them a colorful Finnish Marimekko tablecloth as a wedding gift. They admired its beautiful floral design and bright colors. After playing with the dogs again, they drove north to Marquette.

NOON SKATE

Gena and Kaarina were expecting them at Gena's house for dinner, and they would stay there overnight, being on their guard for more short-sheeted beds. But Brad said it was too early to go there because no one would be home from work, so he took Monica to one of his favorite places, Presque Isle, where he used to go for picnics and family outings as a boy.

At Presque Isle, they watched tankers being loaded with iron ore from the nearby mines and drove over to a nearby breakwater pier that they walked out on, all the way to the lighthouse at the end. This adventure took over an hour and was an easy walk at first, on solid blocks of concrete. Then the concrete portion of the pier ended and the walk turned into a slow climb on jumbles of huge boulders piled together, with the waves of Lake Superior crashing against the rocks. When they got to the lighthouse, which was closed to the public, they sat on a large flat rock and caught their breath, looking out over the lake, the largest of all the Great Lakes as well as the coldest.

As it would take them a half hour to get back to shore, Brad kept glancing nervously at the darkening sky. At the base of the pier there was a memorial for two Northern Michigan University students who drowned in 1988 when a storm took them by surprise and the waves from Lake Superior swept one of them off the pier. The second student died trying to rescue the first. Fortunately, there was no storm in the works today, and Brad and Monica made it back to shore safely. They drove around the rest of Presque Isle Park counting the deer they saw – eleven. By that time, it was five p.m. and they headed over to Gena's house.

Gena was preparing a dinner of fish, scalloped potatoes and carrots, which smelled wonderful. Her husband Andy got home with their daughters, Iris and Violet, ages nine and eleven, who had been at a day camp, and sent them outside to play until dinner was ready. Kaarina and her husband Sam and their children Kalista, Keith and Kerry, ages four, five and seven, arrived and everyone sat down together for the meal. Monica had time to get better acquainted with her new sisters-in-law. The children watched TV after dinner and the adults talked for a while. Gena and Kaarina and their families gave Monica and Brad as a wedding gift, a pair of Finnish *Iittala* candlesticks and a box of various colors of spherical and teardrop shaped candles to go with them. Brad knew they had not been to Finland recently, so he assumed these beautiful gifts (and those from his parents and Patsy) had been purchased at a shop in Marquette called Touch of Finland that sold products from the U.P. and Finland. They packed these gifts carefully so they would survive the trip back to Center City.

Brad and Monica spent an uneventful night sleeping on the pullout couch in Gena's living room, which they made up themselves with linens that Gena provided. Gena and Andy had offered their bedroom but Brad and Monica insisted on the couch. Gena's fluffy cat, Musti, whose name means "black" in Finnish, curled up with them. In the morning, they had breakfast, thanked Gena for her hospitality and drove off, headed for the twin cities of Houghton and Hancock, where they would catch an amphibious seaplane to Isle Royale, their honeymoon destination.

The drive from Marquette to Houghton and Hancock took almost two hours because they got behind a slow truck. Brad drove while Monica watched for more deer along the side of the road, spotting three of them.

In Houghton, Brad drove Monica around the campus of Michigan Technological University, his alma mater, and showed her the ice rink where he had played intramural hockey. "I never played on an organized team," he said. "Just on the lake with the boys when I was growing up, and later here, just for fun. They do have a figure skating club, but I never looked into it."

From Michigan Tech, they drove north to the Houghton County Memorial Airport, parked their car in the long-term lot and checked in with the seaplane company. They purchased snacks from a vending machine and sat down to wait until it was time to board. Brad had chosen the plane over a boat to get to the remote island because he remembered getting seasick on the boat as a boy when his family went to Isle Royale for a camping trip. "The boat, Ranger III, takes up to six hours, and the seaplane, only 35 minutes, so it will be a better use of our time," he told Monica.

There was another couple on the plane, also on their honeymoon and staying at the Rock Harbor Lodge, the closest thing to a hotel on the remote island. The pilot welcomed the two couples aboard and explained that the main island, where the lodge was located, stretched 45 miles in length and up to nine miles across, and there were several smaller islands. The 893 square mile area, established as a national park in 1940, is known for its undisturbed wilderness -- no cars or dogs are allowed.

"Why no dogs?" Brad asked, glad they had not tried to bring Aliina.

"Because they might infect the wolf population with canine diseases," replied the pilot, adding that the wolf population had dwindled to dangerous low numbers anyway.

"Do you think we'll see any moose?" Monica wondered.

"Definitely," the pilot said. "And probably some wolves and beavers, but there are no bears."

That was comforting, Monica thought. All she had to do was keep out of the wolves' way.

The seaplane gave the couples a spectacular view of Lake Superior and the islands as they approached their water landing. Someone from the Rock Harbor Lodge met them at the dock and led them up a path to the lodge, overlooking the lake. Monica and Brad checked in and unpacked in their comfortable room on the second floor. They went back downstairs to see where everything was located, and found the dining room. There was also a gift shop, a snack bar, and a desk for canoe and kayak rentals and sightseeing excursions. They picked up the information and maps of the island and sat down in the snack bar to have a bite to eat, study the literature and plan the five days they would have there.

Monica wanted to take the sightseeing boat first so she could get an idea of where everything was, so they made reservations right away. They decided to go on a short hike that evening after dinner at the lodge, to a place where they could watch the sunset. They planned a longer hike for another day on one of the 165 miles of hiking trails, and weather permitting, they would rent a canoe on one of the other days. They would play the rest by ear and just enjoy their time together.

On the hike that evening they ran into the other honeymooning couple, April and Terry Thompson, but managed to find their own private rock to sit on to enjoy the sunset. The couples hiked back to the lodge together, listening to invisible wolves howling at the moon. They wondered if these wolves were the last ones on the island.

The sightseeing boat the next day took them to Passage Island and the Rock Harbor Lighthouse. April and Terry had the same idea and joined Monica and Brad and many other passengers on the boat. The guide was very knowledgeable about the island and gave them some tips on where to go on their longer hike. She told them to use plenty of mosquito repellent – the bugs were really bad this year. Brad couldn't remember a time when the bugs *weren't* bad in the U.P. and had remembered to pack a supply of mosquito repellent, so he and Monica were well prepared.

The next day, Monica and Brad hiked as far as they could along one of the easier trails, ate a bag lunch from the dining room and carried their trash back to the lodge. They saw four very large unperturbed moose, which ignored them, and a snowshoe hare just off the path.

On their canoe trip, they saw more moose and some

beavers. They ate lunch on a rock and tried to be as quiet as possible to see what animals would appear. They again ran into April and Terry, who had capsized but were unharmed. That evening, the two couples had dinner together in the lodge and compared notes on what animals they had seen and how many mosquitoes had attacked them. They agreed they had all had a memorable time.

Monica enjoyed her time with Brad on this beautiful island where they had no technology to distract them and could relax and just be together (except when they kept running into April and Terry). She was sorry to see it all end when it was time to catch the seaplane back to Houghton County Memorial Airport. However, all morning flights were cancelled that day due to the weather – high winds and three-foot waves. Monica and Brad wandered into the dining room for a leisurely breakfast and several cups of coffee. April and Terry joined them, also stranded.

To kill some time, Monica and Brad went for a long walk and returned in time for lunch. The waves seemed smaller, but there was no word from the pilot. As they were finishing dessert, they heard the seaplane coming in for a landing and figured that flights had resumed. The pilot ran extra flights in between his scheduled ones, and Monica and Brad found themselves flying again with April and Terry.

"All's well that ends well," Brad said, after the amphibious plane landed in Houghton. Everyone thanked the pilot for his extra work, and the couples again said their goodbyes, wondering where they would run into each other the next time.

NOON SKATE

They picked up Brad's car at the airport and drove to Hillside where they stayed with Brad's parents for the night, picked up their dinnerware and Brad's accordion, and headed home to Center City. Brad's parents invited Brad and Monica to come back for Christmas – and to bring Aliina, Suzi and plenty of warm clothing.

They drove for seven hours. Monica was happy to get home and see Suzi and Aliina, who had survived almost two weeks by themselves. The mail had piled up, and Monica and Brad were pleased to find a number of wedding cards from their skating friends, gift cards from Margie and Rose, and a gift check from Monica's parents.

After a nice dinner and catching up with Suzi, Monica and Brad had a glass of wine on the deck in view of the birch and pine trees out back – just like the ones they had seen in the U.P. Monica was sure she could hear the Finnish spirits in the trees, whispering the words or singing to her all the songs she had heard Brad's family playing together. She thought she must be the luckiest person in the world to have found such a wonderful man and his extended family. She couldn't wait for Suzi to meet them all at Christmas time.

Chapter Seven

With the Center City Ice Arena closed until after Labor Day, Monica and Brad still had nowhere to skate and joked about having withdrawal symptoms. Brad used the extra days to catch up on his consulting contracts, and Monica helped Suzi pick out the remaining things on her list for college, including a quilt for her bed and other dorm room decorations. She had ordered her books online and would pick them up at the Winter College bookstore.

On Labor Day, Brad helped Suzi load the Regal with her suitcases, boxes, and bags of college stuff. "I'm really excited for you," he said. "College is great fun, but you do have to remember to study!"

With the car loaded, Suzi sat down with Aliina and told her to be a good dog. "I'll see you at Thanksgiving," she said. "I'm going to miss you so much."

There was no room for Aliina in Brad's car, and he thought it was better that Suzi said goodbye to her at home, anyway, so they drove off with Suzi waving to Aliina out the back window.

When they pulled up to the dorm in Winter Grove 90 minutes later, Brad helped unload the car while Monica found a dolly and Suzi grabbed a cart. They started pushing and pulling Suzi's belongings towards the building while Brad found a parking place. Suzi had to check in at a table set up outside and pick up her keys. They waited for an elevator and loaded everything onto it, stopping at the fourth floor, where Suzi's room was located. Her roommate, Ellie, from Grand Rapids, had already arrived and was unpacking with her mother. Ellie and Suzi had met online through the college website and gave each other a welcoming hug.

Brad came in carrying another box, and everyone introduced themselves. Monica helped Suzi unpack while Brad returned to the car for the rest of Suzi's stuff.

"We'll come up and take you to dinner in October," Monica said. She gave her daughter a big hug and kiss, and told her to study and to text or call at least once a week.

"I will," Suzi promised, "Thanks for helping, Brad. Give Aliina a big hug for me." She gave Brad a hug and said goodbye to him and Monica.

Monica blinked back tears as she and Brad left the dorm room and walked down the hall to the elevator. When they got to the car, she fought to hold back more tears. Once they were on the highway, she couldn't hold them back any longer and started bawling.

"My baby," she said, "I'm so proud of her." She tried to explain to Brad what it was like to leave her only child in a place where she would learn and grow and become an adult, while her role as a parent would grow smaller.

"You will always be her mom," Brad said. "Maybe the relationship will change, but the love will always be there. You are lucky to have each other and I am privileged to be part of your journey with her, from here on, anyway. You know if there is anything I can ever do for Suzi, I will."

Monica reached out and took his hand, still blinking back tears. She was glad she had Brad to hold onto and that she would not be coming back to an empty home.

Aliina kept looking around the house for Suzi for the next few days. She went back to sleeping in Brad and Monica's room, keeping a watchful eye on the door for Suzi.

On Tuesday, Monica left for work. She took her skate bag and told Brad she would see him at noon skate. "Let's see if we remember how to skate," she said. They thought it would take two weeks to get back to where they had been before the break, as it had in other years.

At the office, Monica pulled a pile of papers from her mailbox and opened her email in-box to find hundreds of new messages. It would take her all morning to get caught up. She was happy to learn that a fully executed settlement agreement had been received in the discrimination case filed by job applicant Sarah Ahmed against Bob Ritter. Mr. Ritter's back pay check for Ms. Ahmed and his check to the U.S. government for civil penalties were in Audra's office, and Audra asked Monica to send the checks to Ms. Warren in the Office of Special Counsel for forwarding to Ms.

Ahmed. Monica wrote a cover letter and arranged for the checks to be sent, per Audra's instructions. Monica turned to two new legal research assignments for other attorneys on the fifth floor.

At noon skate, Monica and Brad spent the first half hour working on stroking and edges – forward and backward. They skated all the lower level dances that were played, to get their feet back under them and to try to regain any endurance they had lost. Monica skated the Argentine Tango, which she had already passed, with Brad, and then they both worked on their solos for the Westminster Waltz and the Quickstep. Brad stayed for the general session and Monica returned to the office.

It seemed strange to come home and have dinner without Suzi, who had texted Monica several times during the day with questions about her financial aid package, and whether she had enough money in her bank account to pick up some unanticipated supplies. Monica assured her this was fine and wished her luck on starting her classes.

That night, Monica dreamed she was in college and it was exam week but she had never attended one of her classes. This was a recurring dream that she had not had for a while. "Why am I having this dream?" she asked Brad. "Suzi is the one in college."

Brad said he used to have a similar dream and now he was having one about showing up at an ice dance test session, realizing he had no idea how to do the dance he was about to test. They laughed about how silly this was, but the dreams seemed so real and unnerving. They hoped Suzi wouldn't be having any such nightmares.

On Thursday, Monica and Brad had their lessons with Harvey on noon skate. They compared notes on vacations during the two-week break, and went to work on their dances. Harvey showed Brad how to assist the lady on her twizzle and worked with him on his Argentine Tango solo to make his edges deeper. He skated Monica's two remaining gold dances with her to get back into the swing of things, and watched her solos, reminding her of the judges' comments. "The West just needs mileage," he said. "Skate as many patterns of it as you can, every day."

The Sunday night Center City Skating Club adult ice dance session started up again, bringing all the adult ice dancers of Center City back together. Those who had not seen each other since the spring ice show had a lot of catching up to do during the break. Everyone was a bit rusty except for Callie and Ben, who had gone to Sun Valley, Idaho for the last two weeks of summer break and skated every day on the outdoor ice rink there, where the elevation was almost 6,000 feet. They explained that the outdoor rink had a large canopy over it to shield it from the sun during the day, and the evenings were cold enough that the ice could be maintained, even in the summer. Monica thought it sounded fantastic, and Brad said he would like to go there someday. Callie and Ben, who were getting along well, appeared to have gained strength and endurance from two weeks of skating five hours a day at high altitude.

The test schedule for the Center City Skating Club was posted, showing that the first dance test session would be held in December. That would give everyone three months to prepare for their next ice dance tests. Monica and Brad both hoped to test their remaining gold dances and become gold dance medalists. Janet and Julian were pressuring Monica and Brad to start trial judging and work on getting their bronze dance judging appointments. Monica wanted to do this sometime but didn't think she would have the time to put into it until she passed all of her gold dances. Brad said he would attend the upcoming judges' school and give trial judging a shot in December. He would need to judge a prescribed number of tests with a high percentage of agreement with the actual judges in order to get his appointment.

Lessons with Harvey were going well, and Monica was getting caught up at work. Suzi's calls and texts from college were becoming less frequent as she got into the routine of classes, studying and swim team practice. Brad had gone back to taking Aliina for her morning walks and had been gone about fifteen minutes one morning, when Monica heard Aliina barking loudly, which was unusual for her. The barking was not happy excited barking like when she saw people or other dogs she knew. This was frantic barking, and it was getting louder. Then Aliina was jumping against the back door. Monica was in the kitchen, about to leave for work. She opened the door and did not see Brad anywhere. Aliina kept barking and turned around as if to tell Monica to follow her. Monica grabbed her phone and ran after the dog, hoping that Brad was nearby and maybe helping out a friend.

When she got to the foot of the driveway, Monica saw Brad lying face down in the grass. "Brad!" she screamed, rushing to turn him over and give him an airway like she had learned in a CPR class many years ago. Brad was breathing but unconscious. Monica was terrified and had no idea what was wrong. She dialed 911 on her phone and reported her emergency. She sat with Brad until an ambulance arrived. Aliina sat there, too, licking Brad's face.

Richard, the neighbor who had cared for Aliina when Monica and Brad went to Washington, D.C., came out to wait with them. Monica handed Aliina over to Richard and rode in the ambulance with Brad to get a head start on giving them his information, while they sped off to Central Hospital.

While Brad was being examined, Monica called in to work and said she had a family emergency. Anna, the receptionist, said she hoped everything would be all right and promised to let everyone know that Monica would probably not be in that day. Monica sat in the family waiting area at the hospital, hoping and praying that Brad would be OK. Good grief, Monica thought – they hadn't even been married six months. They were supposed to have the rest of their lives together. There were so many things they wanted to do. Monica had finally found someone she could trust and rely on, after being on her own for so long, and to lose him now was unthinkable. Brad had to be OK!

After about 90 minutes, a doctor finally appeared and told Monica that Brad had been admitted and would be there at least overnight. Thank heavens, she thought, relieved that Brad was alive. "What is wrong with him?" she asked.

Brad had suffered a subarachnoid hemorrhage – a blood vessel had burst under the arachnoid layer of his brain, causing him to have a severe headache and pass out. "Will he be OK?" Monica demanded.

"We will have to wait and see," said the doctor. "He is awake now and we have given him something for the pain. Would you like to see him before he falls asleep?"

The doctor led Monica to Brad's room. He was propped up on some pillows and smiled when he saw Monica. "Wow, I can see both of you," he said. Monica thought he meant both her and the doctor, but he explained that he was seeing two of everything.

"We can order some special glasses for you," the doctor said. "But you will have to be twice as careful." Brad didn't think this was funny and asked how long he would be seeing double.

"Until your brain heals itself," the doctor said. "Just don't fall on your head and you will be fine -- eventually." Brad had visions of falling backwards and hitting his head on the ice but didn't say anything and tried to think of something else.

"What happened to Aliina?" he asked Monica, and she told him about how the dog had come to get her and led her to him. She assured him that the neighbor, Richard, had Aliina and the dog was not out roaming the streets of Center City. Monica sat with Brad until he fell asleep. She took a cab home, picked up Aliina from Richard's and took her to the house, making sure the dog had food and water for the day. Then she drove in to the office. There would be no time for noon skate – she wanted to catch up on work and meet a deadline that she had that day for one of her research assignments. She returned to the hospital in the evening to see how Brad was doing.

He was awake when Monica got there. He had been watching the news and trying to get used to seeing two of everything. That night the Southside Apartments fire was in the news again. The two arsonists had pleaded guilty and had been sentenced to life in prison without the possibility of parole for setting fire to the building which resulted in the death of resident Horace Raines. Monica and Brad were thankful that the two men had taken responsibility for their awful deeds and there would be closure for Horace's family. The TV news reporter went on to cover a few of the families who had survived the fire but were still in need of assistance. Most of the families had moved on and had found other places to live in Center City, or had left the area for a brand-new start somewhere else.

Monica returned to an empty house, except for Aliina, who was now looking around for Brad as well as Suzi. She called Suzi and told her what had happened and not to worry. Suzi worried anyway, truly concerned about Brad, of whom she had grown very fond since he came into their lives. Monica also called Brad's parents to let them know he was in the hospital but would be coming home the next day. Finally, she called Patsy, who was concerned that Brad might have the same condition as her husband, Brad's cousin Don, who had died suddenly in March.

Patsy said, "Aliina might have saved him by coming to get you quickly so you could give him an airway and call for help. It's also very fortunate you have a hospital nearby. We didn't find Don right away and the nearest hospital is in Marquette."

Monica was truly grateful for Aliina's actions and for

Central Hospital. That night, she gave the dog a special dinner and a big hug. Aliina curled up at the foot of the bed, but Monica could not sleep. She worried about Brad and whether he would be able to return to his usual activities, primarily skating. She knew how much he loved it and how he would hate to be off the ice for even a short time. Of course, he had to follow the doctor's orders, but she knew this would be difficult for him. She was just thankful that he was alive and she had not lost him. Whatever his condition turned out to be, she wanted to help him through it, as she knew he would do for her.

Brad was released from the hospital the next day but was not cleared to skate or drive for at least two weeks, until he had an appointment with an ophthalmologist and had received glasses that would help him adjust to seeing double, if he still needed them.

Monica resumed her work and skating schedule but missed Brad on the ice. She took both her lesson time and Brad's time from Harvey, to work on her two remaining gold dances. She treasured her skating time, when she could get her mind off of her problems. By concentrating on each step of the dance she was doing and listening to the music, she could block out everything else.

The next two weeks at work were spent preparing for trial in Linda Baird's diminished value car case. The at-fault driver's insurance company was still refusing to pay Linda for the difference in value between her brand-new car and the value of her car after its front end was completely rebuilt. Monica researched a couple of issues for Wes and sat in on Wes' prep session with Linda, where he went over her earlier deposition testimony and what she could expect in the one day trial in the Center County Courthouse nearby. Wes also touched base with Linda's expert witness on diminished value who would be driving up from Detroit.

Wes asked Audra to help him with jury selection. He had been involved in jury selection on one of Audra's cases and valued her opinion on which jurors should be struck and which ones retained. Audra offered to sit in on the trial after the jury was seated, in case Wes needed anything. Monica would sit at the table with Wes to take notes and pass him any documents he needed during the trial.

After an opening statement, Wes called Linda as his first witness, and she described what had happened in the accident and how she had ended up with a rebuilt car that was worth far less than what she had paid. Linda's expert, Geraldine Long, testified clearly about the type of damage Linda's car had sustained and why its repairs, even if correctly done, made the car worth thousands less.

The insurance company's attorney, Cora Barron, cross-examined Linda and the expert, Ms. Long, without doing any harm, and then called the apparent expert from her own company, Perry Eastman, whose testimony Wes hoped would not be very convincing. On cross-examination, Wes brought out that this expert had very little experience and worked for the same insurance company. The other driver was present but did not testify, as the parties had stipulated that she was at fault.

Both attorneys gave closing statements and the jury was given its instructions. They were led to a room for their deliberations, and Wes, Audra, Monica and Linda went out for coffee and a snack. The jury had been out for only an hour when Wes got a call to come back to the courtroom – the jury had reached its decision.

Everyone took their seats and the judge and jury came in. When the foreman was asked if they had reached a verdict, he said yes. The jury had found in favor of Linda, awarding her the full amount requested. The other driver would have the right to appeal, which Ms. Barron told Wes she was planning to do. Poor Linda, thought Monica. She still doesn't have what is coming to her. The appeal could take another year, but Wes told Linda he would take care of it and eventually she would get her money.

Surprisingly, a few weeks later, just before the deadline for the appeal, Wes received a check from the insurance company for the amount of the verdict. Ms. Barron had apparently consulted with her superiors and decided an appeal would not be worth it. Wes called Linda and told her the wonderful news.

Brad's double vision slowly returned to normal and he was cleared to drive and skate the week before Thanksgiving. Monica took his hand the first time he stepped on the ice. He had been walking in the neighborhood and riding a stationary bike at home to stay in shape, so he was not as shaky as she expected. He worked on stroking and edges, like they had after the summer break, and he skated the lower dances with Monica. She was thrilled that he was back on the ice and enjoyed doing even the Dutch Waltz and the other preliminary dances with him.

Suzi was done with classes on the Tuesday before Thanksgiving and asked if Monica and Brad could pick her up that evening. Her father Randy and his wife Cara in Oregon had invited her to spend the holiday with them, but she had declined, saying maybe next year. "I just want to come home," she said.

Monica and Brad loaded Aliina in the car and drove up to Winter Grove. The husky barked excitedly when Suzi appeared carrying an overnight bag and her computer. Suzi rode in the back seat with the dog snuggled close to her all the way back to Center City. After dinner Suzi went to bed and slept until noon the next day. Aliina slept with her for most of the night, just like old times.

On Thanksgiving Day, Suzi and Brad watched the Macy's Thanksgiving Day parade while Monica prepared dinner for them and her parents, who drove up from Detroit. They joined hands before the meal and each person said what they were thankful for. Monica's parents were thankful for everyone being able to get together and for the wonderful meal that lay in front of them. Monica said she was thankful for Brad's speedy recovery, and he said he was thankful for his new life with her. Suzi said she was thankful that she had survived the fire, was now attending college and had a home to come back to for the holiday. During the meal, she told them all about her classes, her roommate, swimming, and the friends she had made so far. Monica thought it sounded like the first semester was going well.

Sunday night, Monica drove Suzi back to Winter Grove and said, "Let me know when exams are over. If the timing is right, we might be able to pick you up on our way up north."

On Monday, Monica and the other employees on the

fifth floor of Carter Day were summoned to the conference room for a meeting, which they usually had on Tuesday. Ray Carter and Marcia Day were both present, which was also unusual. Everyone wondered what was going on. After the group was assembled, Ray stood up and said he had some bad news. The firm was downsizing and the partners had made an economic decision and let everyone on the fifth floor go, effective December 31, because they were logging the least number of billable hours of all the departments. If anyone wanted to apply for future openings on the other floors, in tax, probate, family law, etc., they were encouraged to do so. Then he left the room.

Monica and her co-workers sat in shock, not believing what had just hit them. What were they going to do now, just before the holidays? Marcia Day was still in the room and tried to offer them a ray of hope. "You will all get a generous Christmas bonus and severance pay," she said. "And if anyone needs a recommendation, don't hesitate to ask." Then she left the room.

"Well that's just great," said Linsey. "So that's why the other paralegal was not replaced. They knew they wouldn't need anyone."

The attorneys left the room, and Monica and Linsey went to Monica's office to talk. Linsey thought this would be a good time to start law school. Monica had looked into what was necessary for applying to law school and knew that they would need to take the Law School Admission Test, or LSAT. She pulled up the website on her computer and looked at the next test date. If they registered now, they could take the test at the end of December, but then it would be too late to apply for the winter semester at Mid-Michigan Law School. "At least we would know if we have the scores," Monica said. "Let's do it. We have nothing to lose."

"That's for sure," Linsey said. Monica thought to herself that maybe by the time she had been accepted to law school, she would have her gold dance medal and be ready for a new challenge. She hoped Brad would be supportive. Three years of law school would not be easy.

With the dance test session coming up in three weeks, Monica skated at noon every day, preparing to test her Quickstep and Westminster Waltz with Harvey. Brad no longer needed his special glasses after two weeks, and was feeling much stronger, but he and Harvey decided to skip this test session. Brad attended the judges' school held at the Center City Ice Arena and learned valuable information about judging and scoring preliminary and bronze tests. The test session would be on a Saturday, and Brad would be trial judging all morning. He hoped he would not revert back to seeing double, saying with a chuckle to Monica, "The testers might look twice as good or twice as bad." She was sure he would be twice as thoughtful.

Monica and Brad were preparing to pick Suzi up from college at noon on Friday, the day before the test session, but she got a ride home with another student from Center City. This saved Monica a three-hour trip and allowed her to practice one more day at noon skate before her gold dance tests on Saturday. Carter Day had its annual Christmas Party that afternoon, but Monica and Linsey were not in the mood for celebrating and neither were the attorneys and support staff from the fifth floor, who would be unemployed in a week. The fifth-floor employees picked up their Christmas bonus and severance pay checks, said goodbye and left early. Monica would not be back, as she had asked for the last two weeks of December off, to go up north with Brad and to take the LSAT.

On Saturday, ice dance test day, Brad reported to the judges' room to pick up a clipboard that Mrs. Anderson, the test chairperson, had prepared for him. Each judge's and trial judge's clipboard had a set of papers with each skater's name and the dance they would be doing on each paper. Brad checked with the schedule he had been given to make sure he had all the necessary papers. He followed the three judges and one other trial judge out to the rink where they sat in a row on a bench behind the boards. He was wearing his warmest coat and his winter boots to keep his feet warm for the hours he would be out there sitting still, except for when the ice was being resurfaced.

Brad watched each skater carefully and judged each test as he saw it, thankfully not doubled. He gave them what he thought would be fair scores and wrote comments that he thought would be helpful, although the testers would never see the trial judges' papers. After three hours of judging, Brad was exhausted from concentrating on the tests and glad he did not have to skate. He was offered lunch with the judges, so he sat down with Janet and Julian who had just arrived and would be judging the silver, pre-gold and gold dances in the afternoon.

"We are so happy to see you," Janet said. "We need more knowledgeable judges. How was your agreement with the real judges this morning?"

Brad hadn't checked, but when he did, he was pleased that he had agreed with the outcome on all but two of the tests, which he had passed but the real judges had failed with a split panel. He would get some credit for agreeing with the minority judge, at least, and he was well on his way to becoming a credentialed bronze dance judge. He put his coat back on and went out to watch the higher tests and wait for Monica to get there. He wouldn't miss her dances for anything.

Monica had been doing errands all morning and making some last-minute repairs to her black skating dress. She told Suzi this might be her last time to see her mother test her gold dances, so Suzi decided to come to the rink. They got there in plenty of time and found Brad in the stands. Suzi sat down next to him while Monica gave him a hug and went off to put on her skates and stretch for a few minutes before the Quickstep testers had to get on the ice to warm up.

Harvey had only one other student testing the Quickstep, so he did one pattern with each skater in the warmup period. Monica was first to test her Quickstep. She was nicely warmed up and not tired at all, and felt like the dance went well. Her solo also felt good. Brad and Suzi gave her a thumbs up from the stands.

On her Westminster Waltz test, Monica felt like she skated better than the last time, when all of the judges failed her, but she wasn't sure about the solo. She had skated the best she could, so now she would just have to wait for the results.

Mrs. Anderson appeared and gave the test papers to Harvey. He looked them over and gave Monica her results first. She had passed the Quickstep by all three judges but failed the West again.

"You got one pass on the West," Harvey said brightly. "That's better than last time. You are making progress! One more dance to go." He was very pleased with his student, and Monica was happy to have one more dance out of the way. Now she could work with Brad on his Quickstep and Argentine Tango and just worry about one more dance of her own. And the LSAT. She hadn't mentioned this idea to Brad, although she had told him about the layoffs at Carter Day. He told her not to worry about the layoff – something good would come of it, he said, and she would be just fine.

Brad took Monica and Suzi out to lunch to celebrate Monica's passing the Quickstep. "How do you think your exams went?" he asked Suzi.

She groaned and said she had studied all the wrong things and hoped she had answered enough questions correctly to get decent grades, which would be posted online in a few days. Suzi asked to be dropped off at the Center City Mall, where she was planning to meet up with Gail and Alexis, her friends from high school, and do some Christmas shopping. "I can't wait to see them," she said.

Brad found a CD from his sister Gena when he got home – she had mailed it with a request for him to learn as many of the songs as he could so he could play with them at a holiday dance in Ishpeming, a nearby town. The CD contained Finnish Christmas music that he had heard before but had never played. One of the songs was a *jenkka*, or schottische. He grabbed Monica and said, "I'll show you the *jenkka*." He went over the steps: one, two, three, hop; one, two, three hop; then eight hops or pivots. He put Monica on his right side and led her through the basic step, which she picked up right away. They tried it a little faster and then Brad put on the music. They danced around the room with Aliina looking on and staying out of their way.

"You've got it," Brad said. "Now we can have some fun at the dance. I would rather dance than play the accordion, so maybe I will learn one or two new songs and let dad and Gena do most of the work. They have other friends who can play with them. Kaarina and I were never the musicians that dad and Gena were." Monica remembered that Gena was a music teacher in Marquette and taught private violin lessons during the summer at a music camp for children at Northern Michigan University.

Monica and Brad had two days to finish their Christmas shopping. They went to the Center City Mall together to pick out gifts for his parents and other family members. Monica ordered a gift basket of fruit and cheese for her parents and purchased a gift card for Suzi at her favorite clothing store.

"Let's bring our old skates," Brad said. "We may be able to skate on Hillside Lake if they have cleared off the snow." They packed up the car and left Center City on Tuesday, December 22. Suzi rode in the back seat with Aliina while Monica drove up I-75 and across the Mackinac Bridge. Suzi had never been across the bridge and was amazed at how beautiful it was, and how high it was at the top of the span. They stopped for pasties at a small restaurant, dousing them with plenty of catsup. Suzi took Aliina for a walk in a nearby park, where the dog enjoyed leaping through the snow. Then Brad took over the driving on the two-lane roads. They could see that the U.P. had gotten plenty of snow – the snow banks on the sides of the road were six feet high in some places, where the snowplows had been along to clear the road.

They were a half hour away from Hillside when it started raining. Suddenly, the temperature dropped and the rain turned to ice, causing every car on that part of the road to start sliding. Brad's car, with its trunk full of luggage and gifts, spun to the left, the rear of the car going off to the right. "Hold on!" he yelled to Suzi, who was napping in the back seat. He held on to the steering wheel but there was nothing he could do. The car was spinning around. Monica closed her eyes and held on to her seat.

When the car came to a stop, Brad said, "Is everyone OK?"

Monica opened her eyes and found Aliina in her lap – the dog had flown from the back seat. Aliina barked and Suzi sat up, rubbing her eyes. "Yeah, what happened?" Suzi asked. Fortunately, she had been belted in. The car had spun completely around, landing in a snow bank – if not for the huge pile of snow, they would have ended up wrapped around a tree.

Other cars had spun off the road in front of them and behind them. Brad pulled out his phone and tried to call for a tow truck but could not get a signal. Monica and Suzi tried their phones with the same result. They sat in the warm car which was getting colder by the minute and waited until a police car appeared. The state police officer told the drivers of all the vehicles that tow trucks were on the way and they would be pulled out soon.

After about thirty minutes, one of several tow trucks pulled Brad's car out of the snow bank. Brad paid the driver and got a receipt that he would submit to his insurance company, and they were on their way to Hillside. There was so much snow that Monica wondered how Brad knew where he was going – everything looked the same, all covered with white. It was beautiful, though.

When they could get a cell phone signal again, Brad called his parents to let them know they were going to be a bit late. He planned to stop at Patsy's first and let Aliina off, where she would stay with the other dogs. Monica called Patsy to let her know they were on their way despite having been stuck in a snow bank.

When they pulled up to Patsy's, a dozen huskies ran out through the snow to greet them with a chorus of barking. Aliina jumped at the car windows, barking excitedly. Suzi laughed and opened the car door so Aliina could join her canine friends. The dogs got acquainted and the humans went in the house to get warm and have some hot chocolate before driving to Brad's parents' house, where they would stay until the day after Christmas.

"You all look great!" Patsy exclaimed. "It's nice to meet you, Suzi. I'll work with Aliina a little today to see what she remembers about pulling the sled and running with other dogs. Come back tomorrow and we'll take the dogs out to the lake." Patsy explained that a track had been cleared for sled dog teams to run on, and there would also be ice-skating there if Brad and Monica were interested. "I would love to see you guys skate," she said. "And I will take the dogs and whoever wants a ride in the sled – my kids will come, too."

Suzi thought this sounded like great fun. She said goodbye to Aliina, who was frolicking with the other dogs, and got back in the car for the short ride to Brad's parents' home. Arthur and Myra were thrilled to see Brad and Monica, and to meet Suzi. Myra had just baked coffee bread and Christmas cookies, which smelled wonderful. She invited everyone to sit down at the kitchen table for coffee.

After catching up a bit, Monica and Suzi helped Brad unload the car and haul everything upstairs. Suzi would sleep in Kaarina and Gena's old room, and Brad and Monica in his old room. Myra had redecorated the rooms years ago and they no longer resembled children's rooms – instead, they were tastefully decorated for whatever guests they had. Brad and Monica checked the wrapping and tags on the presents and carried them downstairs to put under the beautifully decorated tree that had been cut from the forest nearby. Suzi and Monica admired the tree and the many festive decorations in the house.

Myra told them that dinner would be at six o'clock, and if they wanted to take a nap to recover from their trip, that would be fine. Suzi had already had a nap in the car and wanted to sit by the tree and catch up on her email and Facebook on her laptop. Brad and Monica went upstairs for a much-needed nap. They were thankful to have arrived in one piece after spinning out on the icy road.

For dinner, Myra had prepared beef stew, tossed salad and rolls. Monica and Suzi set the table and everyone enjoyed the meal together.

CAROL MACKELA

In the morning, Brad and Monica dressed warmly, telling Suzi to do the same. He and Monica grabbed their old skates, which they would use to skate on the lake because they did not want to ruin their new blades on the rough outdoor ice. They drove over to Patsy's and helped her load the sled onto a trailer and the dogs into the back of a truck that would pull the trailer. Aliina followed the other dogs and seemed happy to be going on an outing. When they got to the lake they could see other sled dog teams running around the track on the ice, pulling dogsleds and their occupants behind them. Brad had helped Don and Patsy do this many times and wondered how Patsy managed to do it now by herself. She said there was usually someone around to help, but they had not gotten out much with the dogs yet that winter, and she was grateful for Brad's help.

Soon, the dogs were harnessed in, barking excitedly with anticipation. Patsy told her son Donnie, 12, and daughter Molly, 14, to get on the sled and directed Suzi to get in behind them. They pulled a blanket over their legs and waited for Patsy to get on the back of the sled, release a safety line that was holding the dogs, and tell them to go. Off they went! The dogs loved to run, and Aliina fell right in step with them. Suzi took pictures with her phone as they were pulled around on the snowy track.

Brad and Monica sat down on a log and put on their skates. They followed some other skaters to the middle of a large cleared area for skaters. A dozen other people were skating, most of them struggling to stay upright. Brad took Monica's hand and they stroked around the ice in perfect unison, even though there was no music. They did inside

174

and outside edges, forward and backwards, but gave up on doing any of the dances because the area was the wrong size and there were just enough people to make it hazardous. By the time the dogsled made it all the way around the small lake, Brad and Monica were taking off their skates.

"You looked great!" Patsy said. "I saw you from the sled. Now it's your turn for a dogsled ride, Monica."

Monica let Suzi borrow her skates while Donnie and Molly ran back to the truck to get theirs. Brad and Monica climbed onto the sled, pulled the blanket over them, and Patsy told the dogs to go. Aliina and the other dogs barked excitedly and took off around the lake. Aliina ran happily next to a dog named Pekka, and behind her father, Veikko. She didn't look tired at all. Brad pulled Monica close under the blanket and they enjoyed each other's warmth as they sped around the lake.

"Mom, can Suzi come home with us?" Molly asked Patsy when everyone was loading the dogs and the sled for the trip back to their house. "We have a lot of games and there is nothing for her to do at Uncle Arthur's and Aunt Myra's."

Patsy agreed, inviting Brad and Monica for dinner. "You can collect Suzi then," she said. "Or she can stay the night."

Brad suddenly remembered that this was the evening for the holiday dinner and dance at the hall in Ishpeming, where his dad and Gena would be providing the music, and he was expected to join them for at least a few songs. He agreed to drop off Suzi's bag and computer on their way to the dance hall.

Finding themselves free for the afternoon, Brad and

Monica decided to relax, catch up on email and news, and hang out with his parents. He and his dad practiced a few songs together on their accordions. The band would be playing a mix of Christmas songs and old time Finnish dance music – waltzes, tangos, *jenkkas* and polkas.

When evening came, the accordions were loaded in the trunk of Brad's car and his parents climbed in the back seat. Brad and Monica got in and off they went, first dropping off some things for Suzi, who was staying at Patsy's for the night. Then they drove on to Ishpeming, a town to the west of Marquette where Finns from all over the area would be coming to eat and dance together in the spirit of the holidays. As they entered the hall, they could smell the food being prepared in the kitchen. The tables were set and the musicians gathered in front of the hall to test their instruments and the sound system.

More people kept arriving, and Myra and Arthur seemed to know all of them. Brad found many old family acquaintances and high school friends who were still in the area and had fun catching up with them. He introduced Monica to so many people that she gave up on trying to remember their names. She was glad when it was time to sit down for dinner. Brad's sisters Gena and Kaarina and their husbands arrived, and Gena joined Arthur up front with her violin. Along with a drummer and bass player, they would play some dinner music.

The buffet tables opened, and Monica and Brad followed Myra to pick up a plate and load it with chicken, fish, potatoes, vegetables and many other foods. They were half way through the meal when the band struck up a *jenkka*.

NOON SKATE

"Ready?" Brad asked Monica, who was swallowing a carrot. "Let's do the *jenkka*."

Dozens of couples swarmed onto the large dance floor – the biggest one Monica had ever seen. Brad led her all around the floor, avoiding collisions with the other dancers, and they hopped their way through the *jenkka*. A waltz was next, followed by a tango. Brad took Monica back to their table and invited his mother to dance. She was pleased that he had become such a good dancer, and she was a natural follower. They did two more dances, and then Brad took a break.

His father summoned him up to the band and introduced him to the crowd. Brad picked up his accordion and joined in for two numbers, hoping his mistakes would be drowned out by the rest of the musicians. He got a round of applause for his efforts and returned to the table. He and Monica enjoyed several more dances on the large dance floor. The evening ended with a waltz, and everyone left wishing each other happy holidays.

On the drive back to Hillside, Monica wondered what Suzi and Molly were up to at Patsy's and hoped the girls were having fun. The next evening, the family gathered for Christmas Eve dinner at Arthur and Myra's house. Patsy, Molly and Donnie came over and brought Suzi back. After dinner, they sat in the front room and sang Christmas carols before opening their presents. There were squeals of delight as the children opened their gifts and found toys or other gifts they had asked for. Monica received a beautiful necklace and earrings from Brad. Arthur and Myra gave Monica and Brad a quilt that Myra had made. Patsy gave

Monica and Brad matching coffee mugs that said "Sisu" -- a Finnish word meaning guts, fortitude, perseverance, stamina, courage and determination. Monica thought she would have to drink some coffee from this mug every time she had doubts about a skating test, and before she took the LSAT. She also received from "Santa" two bags of Finnish candy called "Marianne." Monica tried a piece, which was hard peppermint on the outside, with a surprise chocolate center. It was the best candy she had ever tasted.

"*Kiitos,*" she said, having learned the Finnish word for thank-you. "I will have to hide these from myself." She offered the candy to others.

After the gifts had all been opened, the families went to the candlelight Christmas Eve service at a church in Marquette where Gena played the violin with a group of musicians. The Finns wished each other *Hauskaa Joulua* -- Merry Christmas. It had been a wonderful day and Monica had enjoyed it tremendously.

On Christmas Day, they gathered at Gena's house for more presents and a meal together. The next day, Brad, Monica and Suzi loaded up the car for their trip back to Center City, and drove to Patsy's to pick up Aliina. Suzi was happy to have the dog back with her but felt bad when Aliina howled all the way to the Mackinac Bridge. Was she missing the other dogs?

"She always does this," Brad said. "Don't feel too sorry for her, Suzi. She has a loving home and can sleep on a bed with people – not in a barn with the dogs. Patsy can't keep every puppy. Aliina gets her trip up home at least once a year, so that will have to do."

NOON SKATE

Aliina settled down with her head on Suzi's lap and rode in comfort all the way back to Center City. Monica told Brad she was planning to take the Law School Admission Test on Wednesday, and he was surprised but thought that was wonderful. She had ordered a book to prepare from and was planning to study when they got home.

Noon skate was suspended for the holidays and replaced with general public sessions where everyone would be trying out new skates that they got for Christmas, so Brad didn't even try to go and busied himself with his consulting work.

Monica studied the LSAT test preparation book to familiarize herself with the format of the test, which was a test of reading comprehension and reasoning. She hoped she was up to it. On Wednesday, she made sure to bring her admission slip, ID and several pens and pencils with her and set out for the testing room at Mid-Michigan University. She found herself in a large auditorium with over one hundred prospective law school students, all of whom appeared younger than Monica, who was almost 38. She thought that her life experience might prove helpful, at least. Linsey, only a few years younger than Monica, was seated a few rows away. They wished each other luck.

The proctor checked everyone's IDs again and passed out the sealed test booklets. When everyone had a booklet in front of them, they were told to open the booklets, read the directions carefully and begin. There were several timed sections of the test, which Monica completed. The test takers were relieved when it was all over, each one hoping they had done well enough to get into the law school of their choice. "If you think this was bad," said the proctor, "wait until your first law school exam, or the bar exam."

She told the testers that their results would be available online in two weeks, using the password they had set up. Monica and Linsey went out for a drink, figuring they had earned it after a day of testing.

Monica tried to put the LSAT out of her mind and enjoy New Year's Eve with Brad. Suzi went to a party at Gail's, and Brad and Monica went to the New Year's Eve party at the Center City Club. They dressed to the nines and enjoyed an evening of dining and dancing. A big screen TV was set up so everyone could watch the ball drop in Times Square in New York City, and they counted it down together, glasses of champagne in their hands. Brad and Monica kissed and joined in singing "Auld Lang Syne."

Monica couldn't believe the New Year was beginning. She looked forward to skating, passing her last gold dance, and starting law school, if everything worked out. She still had most of the insurance money from the fire and had deposited her checks from Carter Day in her bank account. These funds would cover her tuition for the first two years, she hoped. She knew Brad would help her out, but she hated to burden him since he might end up having to pay some of Suzi's tuition – their household income had increased dramatically with her marriage to Brad, and Suzi was in danger of losing her financial aid, based on need, after the first year at Winter College.

Brad was looking forward to many more years with Monica and thanked his lucky stars every night that she had agreed to marry him. Whether he passed any more dances or not, he knew they would enjoy skating together for many years to come.

Suzi's classes started up again on January 4, and Brad and Monica drove her back to school. She had passed all of her first semester exams with flying colors and had registered for English literature, another psychology class, a history class and an introductory philosophy class. Her roommate Ellie would be back, and the swim team had most of its meets in January and February, leading up to their conference meet in March.

The first week of January felt very strange to Monica – she had no job and Suzi was gone, so Monica had nowhere to go except noon skate. For the first time, she and Brad could go together in one car and stay for the next session to continue working on their dances. The next test session would be on Saturday, January 30.

Harvey worked with Monica on her remaining gold dance, the Westminster Waltz, and with Brad on his three remaining gold dances, which he skated with Monica every day. Harvey signed their test applications for all of these dances.

Monica checked her email several times a day for her LSAT results. She and Linsey were getting nervous. When the results finally came, Monica was relieved to learn she had done very well, as had Linsey. They met for coffee and to plan the next step – getting their law school applications completed and coming up with references. Marcia Day, Audra and Wes had already agreed that both Monica and Linsey could use their names. Audra and Wes were not sure where they would be working and had talked about starting their own firm, but not yet, so Monica and Linsey used the home addresses and phone numbers they had been given. They completed their applications and sent them to Mid-Michigan Law School, located conveniently in Center City. The law school had three semesters a year – students could take ten credits a semester for three semesters, or fifteen credits for two semesters, to finish in the usual three years.

On January 30, Brad opted not to trial judge on the lower level tests in the morning because he didn't want to be worn out before he tested his golds. Monica partnered him through his three dances – the Argentine Tango, the Quickstep, and the Westminster Waltz, which felt good. Then she tested the West with Harvey and skated a strong solo. She didn't know how she could have skated the West any better and hoped at least two of the judges would pass her. Harvey told Brad his dances had all looked good, but they waited nervously for their results anyway.

Mrs. Anderson appeared with an unusually big smile and gave Monica her papers. Harvey was standing there, and he and Monica looked at each paper: Pass, Pass, and another Pass. Whew! She had finally done it, after seven years and countless test sessions and lessons.

"Congratulations!" chorused several of the skaters, as the news spread that Monica was Harvey's newest gold medalist – the fifth one in his seven years at Center City. She would receive a piece of paper from the United States Figure Skating Association signifying her accomplishment. Mrs. Anderson told her that the Center City Skating Club would purchase her gold medal and award it to her at the spring banquet.

Monica was so happy, she had forgotten about Brad for a moment. She hoped he had passed at least one dance. Harvey had just received Brad's papers and told him that he had passed the Quickstep by all three judges and had received one pass on each of the other two dances, so he would need to retake them.

"Not a problem," he said. He was truly happy for Monica, knowing how hard she had worked to get to this point. "Let's go out to celebrate!" he said. They invited Harvey to come along and they went out to dinner.

When they got home and checked the mail, there was a large envelope for Monica from Mid-Michigan Law School. "That looks promising," Brad said. "If they were rejecting you, it would be a smaller, thinner envelope."

Monica ripped the envelope open to find a law school brochure, several other pamphlets about financial aid and campus resources, and a cover letter. She scanned it for the words "accepted" and found them! She had been accepted for the fall semester. The best part was that she had been offered a merit scholarship of 80% of the tuition based on her undergraduate grade point average and her LSAT scores. She couldn't believe it! Mid-Michigan Law School was apparently trying to recruit and retain the best students and would renew the scholarship every semester based on the student's grade point average: a 4.0 would earn 100% of the next semester's tuition; a 3.9 would earn 90%; a 3.8 would earn 80%; and so on. Monica realized that her insurance money and the two checks from Carter Day would fully cover the three years of tuition if she did well.

Monica checked her phone and found a text from Linsey

saying that she had also been accepted at Mid-Michigan Law School, so they would be starting classes together. They had agreed that if they made it through law school and passed the Michigan Bar Exam, they would hang out a shingle in Center City and be their own bosses.

"This has certainly been a successful day," Brad said. "Congratulations! I am so proud of you!" He gave Monica a big hug.

"Can we travel before I start law school?" Monica asked.

"Where do you want to go?" Brad had been taking Monica to all the places he wanted to go, and now he was happy to let her choose the next trip.

"Sun Valley!" Monica said. "In the summer. Then I will be all ready to start law school in the fall."

Brad thought that sounded like a perfect plan.

Appendix -- List of Ice Dances

Preliminary
    Dutch Waltz
    Canasta Tango
    Rhythm Blues

Pre-Bronze
    Swing Dance
    Cha Cha
    Fiesta Tango

Bronze
    Hickory Hoedown
    Willow Waltz
    Ten-Fox

Pre-Silver
    Fourteenstep
    European Waltz
    Foxtrot

Silver
    American Waltz
    Tango
    Rocker Foxtrot

Pre-Gold
    Kilian
    Blues
    Paso Doble
    Starlight Waltz

Gold
    Viennese Waltz
    Westminster Waltz
    Quickstep
    Argentine Tango

Dances may be taken and passed in any order within each level, however, all dances at each level must be passed before the skater may move on to the next test level. Upon completion of all tests above, the skater is deemed a gold medalist in ice dance. For more information, see *Official U.S. Figure Skating Rulebook*, www.usfigureskating.org; and Dyer, Lorna, *Ice Dancing Illustrated*, Moore Publications, Inc., Bellevue, Washington, 1980 (detailed descriptions of ice dance technique, dance positions, steps, turns, and all dances).

55799335R00108

Made in the USA
Middletown, DE
12 December 2017